Of Peace and Precipitation

Of **Peace** and **Precipitation**

———————— Aaron J. Gourlie ————————

Stacia,
May you find hope.

Aaron J. Gourlie

RESOURCE *Publications* · Eugene, Oregon

OF PEACE AND PRECIPITATION

Resource Publications
An Imprint of Wipf and Stock Publishers
199 W. 8th Ave., Suite 3
Eugene, OR 97401

www.wipfandstock.com

PAPERBACK ISBN: 978-1-6667-1098-4
HARDCOVER ISBN: 978-1-6667-1099-1
EBOOK ISBN: 978-1-6667-1100-4

09/20/21

In the rain I bleed,
dripping softly, quietly.
Wash the blood away.

Chapter 1

H er mom was late again. It was the unknown that was most disconcerting to Jen Morris. She never knew when her mother would have some sense of normalcy or act "cray-cray" as her best friend Morgan would say.

Having her own phone would probably be the most useful thing in the world, but here Jen stood the one and only high school student without a phone. Whenever she brought it up to her mom, the reply was some combination of she wasn't "old enough" and they "didn't have the money." She laughed at the old enough excuse as she observed a line of third graders standing outside the intermediate school, faces aglow from their rectangular screens, playing the newest season of Fortnite. Jen knew the "it was too much money" part was probably right, although it seemed they paid more for her mom's "cheaper" pre-paid phone than they would for a *real* phone on a *real* plan.

It was embarrassing being the only phoneless girl in school. Jen settled for her cousin Mario's old iPod Touch that at least resembled a phone. On occasions such as this, instead of standing awkwardly with her hands in her pockets, she'd hold it up to her ear and pretend to be talking to someone or fiddle with it so she looked like she was texting. She wanted to message Morgan but the school's Wi-Fi was too finicky, and she kept getting signed out.

Every passing car brought new hope that her mom was coming to rescue her. Every passing person, whether teacher, administrator, janitor, cheerleader, football or volleyball player, stopped to stare and sometimes ask if she needed help or question why she was still at school. One teacher stopped Jen in the hallway, informing her that the drama club meeting had ended twenty minutes ago and that she needed to go home and wasn't allowed to "linger" at school. The teacher squinted at her suspiciously when Jen explained her mom was coming and should be there any minute.

As if I want to stay this late, because school is sooo amazing . . . Jen thought.

Uggghh . . . Where is she? It's hard enough going to a new school without the upperclassmen looking at you as if they could catch the uncool disorder all ninth graders have, unless they're really pretty or really good at sports.

Jen felt that since she was in no way an exceptional athlete (although she was a decent tennis player) nor exceptionally good-looking, it was best to remain anonymous until the eleventh grade or so. No thanks to her mom, being the weird girl that stays after school to hang out by herself didn't qualify as anonymous. She knew her mom, flaws and all, did care about her. Her little brother Ronnie was pretty cool too, usually, when he wasn't hogging the TV with endless video games. But right now, she just wanted to get home and *not* be on display.

Jen normally rode the bus, but had stayed after school that day for "an hour-long informational meeting" about the upcoming school play. It had consisted of Mr. Doss showing up thirty-some minutes after the meeting was supposed to start, telling the students they had not yet decided on the play, handing them flyers that said, "School Play To Be Announced, Auditions: September 23," and promptly leaving.

Wow, that was worth it. I seriously stayed after school for that? Jen thought as the meeting ended.

The main drama teacher had left after the first week of school. Mrs. Borowsky put in her thirtieth year of teaching last June. Although she qualified for the full benefits of retirement, she told the administration her love of teaching was too strong to retire. Then, after exactly one week, five full days into the new school year, she decided to retire. It left the school scrambling to find a replacement. Supposedly, they had hired someone and they were to start next week. Without an actual theater teacher, Mr. Doss was left to run the meeting. It was not surprising that the school had postponed the announcement of the fall play, but it would have been nice to at least hear something about the new teacher, or what plays they were considering, or what auditions would be like, or *anything*. All Mr. Doss really did was show up.

Then, again, Mr. Doss had never spoken a word more than was necessary. Jen had no idea how Mr. Doss ended up being part of the theater department. He was ginormous physically, like 6'2" or 6'3" and over 250 pounds, mostly muscle. He was the wrestling coach, an assistant football coach, and a physical education teacher. He had been a wrestler at Iowa State and was probably the least theatrical adult in the school. Carl, the maintenance man, could at least whistle a tune. For Mr. Doss, it seemed to be a chore to even speak. Jen wondered if being part of the drama program was part of a community service sentence or a condition of his parole. Jen couldn't imagine Mr. Doss doing anything to help a play except maybe to keep everyone in order. He did excel at that.

Jen's mom, Lana, came twenty-five minutes after she was supposed to, which meant more than forty-five minutes had passed since the theater meeting had ended. Jen's mom pulled her partly rusted, partly dented, early nineties, white Subaru station wagon into the parking lot very slowly.

Lana could be spotted from innumerable distances by the rate in which her car moved. She often had a line of cars behind her beeping, as if she was the lead vehicle in a slow car parade. This drove Jen's best friend Morgan crazy. Jen had become so accustomed to her mom's driving that she barely noticed how slow she drove. It was much more obvious to Morgan. Morgan insisted on her mom driving everywhere since Lana's driving was maddening to her.

Lana pulled up with Ronnie riding shotgun. Jen aggressively opened the rear passenger door, jumped in and yelled: "Mom! What took you so long!? I've been waiting for almost an hour!"

"Don't you talk to your mother like that!"

"Mom, I've been waiting for a long time!"

"I'm sorry but your brother let Fifi out."

"Mom, Fifi will be fine! She'd be fine for fifteen minutes!"

"You remember the last time you let her out, we couldn't get her back for four hours. You know Fifi has arthritis."

"I swear you love that cat more than me!"

"That's not true, but you know Fifi is an important part of this family. She's like your sister."

"Mom, the cat is *NOT* my sister. It's a stupid cat!"

"Jen! Don't you dare talk about Fifi like that! She loves you."

"I'd loved to kick her," Jen muttered under her breath.

"Mom! Jen just said she'd love to kick Fifi!" Ronnie quickly interjected.

"I did not!"

"JEN!" Lana said shocked.

"You did too! You did!" Ronnie quickly turned to his mother: "Mom she really did!"

"Ronnie! Shut up! Shut up! You're an idiot, Ronnie!"

"Jen! What is wrong with you!? You wouldn't talk like that in church!"

"Yes I would!"

"Don't you dare say another word missy! I can't believe you. I just don't understand you! No TV when you get home! Or talking on the phone to Morgan! You're grounded!"

"I'm grounded because you can't be on time?"

"You know I had to get Fifi. I don't want to hear another word about it! I don't even know you anymore, Jennifer!"

"No, you really don't."

Chapter 2

B reakfast was cold. Cereal. Just the way Jen liked it. This way her mom couldn't burn anything and then be upset when Ronnie and Jen wouldn't eat it. Lana wasn't a terrible cook, but she could be easily preoccupied with other things and forget about something burning on the stove, or it could slip her mind to add essential ingredients like salt or sugar. When she was on, though, Lana's cooking was quite good. As Ronnie tipped his bowl to his mouth and drank the rest of his cereal-flavored milk, Jen wondered what she would do this weekend. Hopefully, she could go to Morgan's house. Morgan's house was like therapy for Jen, a refuge from the craziness of her own home, especially in the summer when Robbie Sutton, Ronnie's friend from down the street, would invade the Morris's household on a daily basis. Her little brother would act even more ridiculous than usual.

"Mom, I think I might spend the night over Morgan's house tonight."

"Jen, you're supposed to be grounded. Plus you have a dentist appointment in the morning."

"Mom, I was only grounded yesterday. You didn't say anything about this weekend. And my appointment is next Saturday, not this Saturday."

"No Jen, I'm pretty sure it's tomorrow. You were just at Morgan's house last week."

"Mom, it's next week and I was only at Morgan's to do some school shopping."

"Jen, I know your appointment is tomorrow."

"Mom, check the calendar."

Lana walked over to the calendar and brushed her index finger across the week to Saturday's date, and then to the next Saturday.

"Well, okay, but I know it was this weekend. I think I wrote it on the calendar wrong."

"Mom, you didn't. It's next weekend. Call the number." Jen pointed to the dentist's card stuck to the almond colored fridge by a pink pearlescent butterfly magnet. As Lana stood by the fridge, Jen re-noticed her mom's pretty blond hair. Lana was about 5'5," curvy with pretty features. Despite being barely thirty-five, she had this way of dressing twenty years older than she actually was. While she didn't have much money to spend on clothes, it was more how she wore the clothes than the clothes themselves. She would tuck shirts in that shouldn't be tucked. She loved sequins and lace and even managed to find them on T-shirts. She would always wear her pants so high on her waist that it almost seemed like a joke. She had a collection of shoes that looked like they were from either a 1970s nurse supply store or from a 1980s prom. She always had strange accessories that somehow looked old but not in the cool retro-hipster sorta way. Lana also had this funny habit of wearing eye shadow that matched her shirt. It made her pretty face oddly colorful. It was as if she was a pretty woman that was stuck inside a costume store. No matter how much Jen or Lana's sister, Julie, tried to help with her look, Lana would say, "That's not my style." Lana seemed to be the only one on the planet that could accurately describe what that was.

Lana checked each digit as she dialed the number and asked the dental receptionist when Jen Morris's appointment was scheduled. The frown that followed told Jen she was right.

"I'm sorry, Jennifer. I really thought your appointment was tomorrow."

"No, it's okay. So I'll probably come back to get some of my stuff before I go over to Morgan's."

"Okay, but I might be at the grocery store when you get home. I have to stop after work and get a few things."

"That's fine, Mom. Just remember we only have eighty-three dollars in our bank account so don't spend any more than sixty dollars."

Despite being fully eligible for the state food assistance program, Lana refused to sign up for it because as Lana's mom used to tell her before she passed, "You have to work for everything you get." Jen thought this was ridiculous since their family really did need the assistance.

"I thought we had more than that," Lana answered in disbelief.

"No, Mom. Not after we paid all the bills. That has to last us until next week when you get paid. So don't buy seventy dollars worth of groceries if you still need gas in your car for next week."

"The bus is here! The bus is here! The bus is heeeerrreee," Ronnie interjected, his voice becoming more and more song-like as he spoke.

Grabbing her books and bag, "Okay, Mom. I gotta go!" Jen said.

"Love you, Jennifer. Love you, little Ronnie."

"Love you too," Jen answered nonchalantly.

"I'm not little!" Ronnie protested yelling over his shoulder.

"You'll always be my little boy!" Lana yelled back as Ronnie ran down the driveway to the bus.

The bus was a means of transportation and nothing more to Jen. Some people really enjoy riding the bus, talking and joking with their friends until they get to school. Jen was not one of those people. Jen didn't really mind the actual bus too much. It was just all the people on the bus. Jen and Ronnie sat towards the front, Ronnie with Robbie Sutton and Jen by herself. Ronnie and Robbie were a funny pair to sit next to each other. They were best friends with similar likes, interests, and personalities, but they were so different physically you wouldn't even know they were in the same grade. Ronnie was slightly small for his age and Robbie was what Jen described as "freakishly tall" for being only in fifth grade. Robbie was about three inches taller than Jen and since Jen was about 5'7" that put him at about 5'10" at age eleven, and made him about nine inches taller than Ronnie.

Jen enjoyed being alone with her thoughts in the morning. Ignoring the more obnoxious students in the back of the bus and just staring out the window was calming for Jen. Now that she was in high school, Jen was less intimidated by the students in the back of the bus, and more annoyed. From time to time, they would call out to her. The culprits were usually one of two guys, both small for being in eleventh grade, but big for riding the bus. They would either make fun of Jen for what she was wearing or accuse her of being too good for them and inevitably call her a nerd for sitting towards the front. Jen learned early in junior high to ignore the people in the back of the bus, instead of humoring or responding to them.

This morning they were focused on the release of the newest Elder Scrolls game update and Jen was left to peacefully put her knees on the seat in front of her and slouch back against the dark green vinyl seats and watch the sunlight filter through the trees and houses along the route. She soon became preoccupied thinking about school. It was a little intimidating being in ninth grade with so many students so old and (usually) more mature than Jen. Jen wondered what it would be like to be a senior. There would be no one to look down on you because you were too young or to laugh if your clothes weren't the newest style. You would run the school, and be the top of the food chain. As much as Jen was ready to be done with eighth grade, there was something nice about being the oldest and coolest students in the school. Now as a freshman, Jen felt insignificant. The bus stopped and Jen stepped across the grated rubber floor down the center aisle. She hopped down the two steps and headed to first period class.

First and second periods usually flew by due to pure busyness. Massive amounts of classwork and homework made first period Algebra go quickly, even if it did take half the period for her brain to fully function. English was all grammar this early in the year, which meant there were thirty-some sentences that had to be re-written correctly. Mrs. Gannon threatened that she would add five sentences per complaint, after some of the students whined that their hands ached. Jen's class quickly quenched their complaints upon hearing that yesterday's fifth period class received fifty sentences. Even Jen's hand ached after correcting the thirty compound-complex sentences. She was relieved her class was smart enough not to complain.

Jen got to spend time with Morgan during third period. It was a bright spot in her schedule. Even though World History wasn't all that exciting, Morgan made it worthwhile. Morgan and her were nearly inseparable in junior high. They had almost identical junior high schedules and sat by each other in every class but one. Jen and Morgan shared most interests and had a similar quick wit and sarcastic humor. After spending most of the summer together, Jen was disappointed to find out that Morgan was only in two of Jen's classes, and one of them wasn't until next semester. They didn't even share the same lunch this year.

Morgan slipped into Room 203 just seconds before the bell rang. Jen noted that Morgan looked very stylish this year, her blond hair cut shorter, with uneven layers of pink streaks and strands that lay perfectly across her face. She looked as if she could be a rockstar. Jen felt like Morgan's hair made her own straight brown shoulder-length hair seem a little boring. Morgan had always dressed more chic than Jen. She always had a bit more money to spend on school clothes and her taste was trendier than Jen's. Morgan was self-assured and confident while Jen didn't really wear makeup and tended to feel awkward in social situations. Jen was grateful for Morgan and her keen fashion sense. Morgan was happy to help Jen pick out new clothes, even with a limited budget. Today, Morgan looked especially good with her ripped, thin but not quite skinny jeans and sky blue American Eagle T-shirt. Jen felt a little cooler just by sitting near Morgan today.

Mr. Harris had been teaching about the various continents in World History. Same stuff just going into a little more detail than Mr. Good taught in sixth grade. Although Jen thought World History was somewhat interesting, all she could think about was hanging out with Morgan after school, and when she would be able to ask if Morgan could have her over. Morgan almost always wanted to hang out with Jen, but once in a while, Morgan's mom would plan some family activity and even Jen wasn't allowed to tag along. Even though this only happened a couple times a year, Jen was scared that this would be the one weekend she wouldn't be allowed to come to Morgan's.

As Jen's mind wandered, the other students' minds seemed to wander too. She began to notice more and more people talking to their neighbors. Still, she didn't want to be interrupted when she finally got to talk to Morgan so she waited for Mr. Harris to finish. Finally, Mr. Harris ceded his lecture to the talkative class and gave the homework assignment.

Morgan quickly turned to Jen.

"Oh my gosh could that be more boring?!"

"Morgan, say that quieter. Mr. Harris might hear you."

"I hope he does. Maybe he'll finally make the class more interesting."

Jen laughed. " I didn't think it was that bad, but I do have something very important to ask you."

Morgan gave a little laugh and said, "Okay. Shoot. Oh, and are you coming over tonight or what?"

"Oh my gosh, I could cry. I'm sooo glad you asked! I needed to have bff time tonight!"

Morgan laughed again and responded, "Geez Jen, you act like you never see me."

Jen noticed a boy staring, almost drooling, at Morgan. Morgan noticed Jen's strange look over her shoulder and turned to see a boy wearing a black Metallica T-shirt gazing at her.

"Can I help you?!" Morgan responded with the right amount of attitude.

"Yeah, I have a question? Were you in Camp Rock? It's an old Disney movie."

"Yeah I know what it is," Morgan interrupted. "No, I wasn't in that movie," she added, annoyed.

"You sure? I swear I saw you in that movie. You look like you want to be a rockstar," the boy said with a mocking smirk that rivaled the Cheshire cat's.

"Yeah, and you definitely look like a movie director. And what's your name?"

"Jordan."

"Okay good. I just wanted to know so when people ask me who that annoying kid is in World History, I can tell them Jordan."

Jen laughed and even clapped in admiration of her best friend.

"CAMP ROCK! Woooo!" Jordan said obnoxiously loud, while putting his rock fist in the air.

Mr. Harris looked up from his desk, rolled his eyes, and shook his head annoyed by the pointless and loud interjection.

Morgan turned around to ignore him again and said to Jen, "What's wrong with these kids?"

"I think that's what all the teachers are wondering."

Chapter 3

The bell rang and as Jen wriggled her hips through the rows of desks to be the first one out of class, her heavy backpack slipped off her shoulder and pendulum swung into a girl with a "420" hoodie, knocking her back.

"Really!?", the girl said with a face that looked like she was ready to throw down.

"Sorry!", Jen yelled over her shoulder as she advanced within a few steps of the doorway. Jen almost stopped to apologize but was unsure if she should pause and have awkward apologetic dialogue at the crowded exit or just keep going. She was in the hallway before she got a chance to decide so she kept walking.

"Watch where you're going ya crazy . . . ", Jen had turned the corner before the girl was able to finish her sentence.

She moved past the final group of people and bolted out of the building and sprinted to her bus. She knew she probably looked crazy running to her bus but did not care. She needed time with Morgan. She felt fortunate to be one of the last students picked up in the morning by her bus and one of the first to be dropped off in the afternoon.

After walking Ronnie to Robbie Sutton's house, Jen headed home to 203 Vine St, a white cape cod with green shutters. Lana had inherited the house from her mother, Jen's grandmother, since Lana's only sibling, Julie, lived in Michigan. Jen was only two when her grandma passed but she had heard a lot about her from Lana's stories and a plethora of odd phrases that didn't translate well to this millennium like "I have a bone to pick with you," "He thinks he's the cock of the walk," and "That'll put hair on your chest" (which was usually applied to Ronnie but once in awhile to Jen, which always brought a scrunched face and "Ew").

Jen unlocked the door and ran up to her room to put together an overnight bag. With excitement, Jen made sure that she packed some of her coolest and most Morgan-approved outfits. She especially appreciated those clothes that were donated to her from Morgan. They were always so nice and were often from brands Jen couldn't usually afford. Morgan bought so many clothes and gave so many to Jen, that Jen wondered if Morgan sometimes purposely bought clothes a size too big since she and Morgan were about two sizes apart. After packing, Jen spent the next ten minutes watching vigilantly for Morgan's mom at the front window.

As soon as she caught sight of Mrs. Neubauer's two year old Nissan sports sedan, she sprinted for the back door. Fifi screeched and jumped up on the kitchen table, avoiding Jen who'd almost stepped on her. Rolling her eyes at the offended cat, Jen barely caught sight of the note from Lana on the kitchen table. Jen froze in her tracks to at least read the note before she exited.

> Jen,
>
> *I'm at the store. Be home at 4pm. If I don't see you before you go, say thank you to Mrs. Neubauer for me. Don't worry, I won't spend more than $80.*
>
> *Love you so so so much Jenny Marie,*
>
> *<3 Mommy <3*
>
> *P.S. Call if you need anything.*

Jen felt the blood flush from her face. *Mom, sixty dollars, Mom! Not eighty dollars! We're going to overdraw our bank account again! We talked about this! Ugh!* Jen quickly grabbed the phone, irritated that Morgan's mom was waiting for her, but more irritated knowing that Lana would probably not answer her cell phone and use her expensive prepaid minutes.

Jen knew what she had to do, but hated she had to do it. She reached for the door, locked it behind her, and walked begrudgingly towards Morgan's car. As she sat in the car, closing the door behind her, Morgan read Jen's clear body language.

"Are you okay?!"

"Yeah, I'm fine," Jen said sternly and emotionlessly.

"No, you're not," Morgan rebutted.

"Yes, I'm fine," Jen said with shortness.

"Is it something with your mom?" Morgan asked with concern.

"No, it's fine," Jen said, turning to Mrs. Neubauer, who also looked concerned.

"Mrs. Neubauer, do you mind stopping at Save Mart on the way to your house? I'm sorry. I just have to talk to my mom real quick and she's at the store. I'm sorry."

"Yeah, of course, that's fine," Mrs. Neubauer replied nonchalantly.

"Thank you."

Morgan, piqued with curiosity, asked in a near whisper, "What happened? Is everything okay?"

"Yes, it's fine. I just need to talk to my mom real quick," Jen said, attempting to be firm but more kind than a second ago.

This is so embarrassing. Why do I have to do this stuff? Why can't I just have a mom like Mrs. Neubauer?

The rest of the six minute trip to Save Mart was silent. As the car pulled into the Save Mart parking lot and Jen saw her mom's Subaru, she leaned toward Mrs. Neubauer and said, "I'll be right back."

Jen didn't worry Lana might be finished shopping and already through the checkout. Jen knew all too well how slowly her mom shopped. She felt frustrated she had to be there at all.. *Why can't my mom be normal?* It was a question Jen asked often, for the last several years now. As she power-walked through the exit know-ing it would be quicker than the entrance, she passed a few empty registers, and strode perpendicularly to the aisles to cover as much ground as possible. Every step aggravated Jen further. Aisle nine? No. Aisle eight? Aisle seven . . . six . . . five . . . four? No. Aisle three held Lana picking her favorite brand of generic Raisin Bran off the shelf. Catching sight of her mom, she rapidly turned and the edge of her favorite faded Gap T-shirt caught the corner of the sale shelf display. It scratched her side and slightly ripped her shirt. Jen cringed from the pain and further agitation, but barely slowed her pace. Twenty feet away, Jen began shouting,

"Mom! Mom!" Lana slowly began to look up. "Mom!"

"Jen? What are you doing here?" Lana said, looking very surprised.

"Mom! I was calling for you!"

"What? What's wrong Jen? Why are you here? I didn't get a call. Is everything alright? Is there something wrong with Ronnie?"

"No, Mom, it's you that there's something wrong with."

"What's wrong Jen? I don't understand. Why are you here?" Lana looked confused.

"Mom! What did we talk about this morning about money?"

"What? Yeah, you said not to spend more than sixty dollars at the grocery store today."

"Sixty dollars! Are you kidding me? Sixty dollars!"

"Yeah, isn't that how much you told me I could spend?"

Jen's face flushed with anger, "Yes, Mom, it is!" Jen's voice seethed with muted anger.

"Why are you so upset, Jen?"

Jen almost began yelling again and showed her teeth trying to hold it back. "I'm upset because you wrote eighty dollars, not sixty dollars!! You said you weren't going to spend more than eighty dollars! Not sixty dollars!"

"No it's sixty dollars not eighty dollars."

"Yes, Mom, I know! You were the one who wrote eighty dollars!"

"Are you sure I wrote eighty dollars? I know it wasn't eighty dollars. It is sixty dollars."

"Yes, I'm sure, Mom! I wouldn't be here if you wrote sixty dollars."

"Well, I don't understand why you're so upset. I knew it was sixty dollars."

"Mom! No you didn't. You don't understand. You don't understand anything! That's why my life is so hard! How many times has Aunt Julie had to come bail us out because we overdrew our checking account?!" Jen said, lowering her tone of voice in an attempt to exit the conversation and leave. "It's fine. You know to only spend sixty dollars. I'm going to go to Morgan's now."

"Well, I'm sorry you thought that, and I'm sorry that I wrote the wrong thing. I thought I wrote sixty dollars."

"It's fine, Mom. Morgan and Mrs. Neubauer are waiting in the car."

"Okay, well have fun. I'm sorry, Jenny. I love you."

Without answering, Jen turned and restarted her power-walk. She raced by the registers, ducking behind racks of magazines, gum, and candy bars hoping no one would see the tears beginning to drip from her face. As she neared the sliding exit doors, it struck her that Morgan and Mrs. Neubauer were still waiting in the car. Jen abruptly stopped at the automatic sliding doors, causing the two shopping carts following her to almost collide. She glanced back at the annoyed shoppers and then hopped through the first of the two sets of sliding doors, quickly sidestepping almost dance-like to the right to alleviate the traffic jam, and let the carts go by. Jen pretended to look at the bubble gum and cheap toy dispensers, while trying to stop the tears still flowing down her face. Her mom made her so frustrated: "Why are you so upset?" Her mom's words echoed in her head. *You could never understand why I'm so upset, that's why I'm upset. You don't know how hard you make my life. That's why I'm upset! I just wanted to hang out with Morgan, and not have to deal with this.* Jen knew her mom was oblivious to how abnormal their life was. She knew her mom. She knew what she was like. Jen felt like she was better than this. Although she was still really annoyed with her mom, she did feel a little bad about how she had talked to her, whether her mom caught how condescending she was being to her or not. Jen took a deep breath, wiped away the remaining tears and took a quick trip to the grocery store bathroom hoping it was cleaner than it turned out to be.

Several minutes later, Morgan and her mom were still waiting patiently in the car, air conditioning running strong on the warm mid-September, Friday afternoon. Jen opened the car door dreading the inquisition that was sure to follow her random necessity to stop at the store and meet her mom.

"Are you okay?" Morgan asked cautiously not wanting Jen to be short with her again.

"Yeah, I'm fine. I just had to make sure my mom didn't forget any groceries," Jen answered in a voice that was much calmer than it was on the way to the store but not really believable.

"Okay, well let's get going girls. Morgan . . . eh hemmm . . . '' Mrs. Neubauer prompted in a not subtle manner, then stared at Morgan in her rearview mirror.

Morgan took her cue: "Jen, I'm sorry I was being nosey . . . ya know about stuff between you and your mom."

"No, that's okay," Jen replied, smiling trying to not get emotional out of admiration for her best friend.

"So what do you want to do today?" Morgan asked in a peppy subject-changing manner.

"I don't care. Whatever you want," Jen answered in a tone that was very pleased to be on a different subject.

"Let's just chill and have some BFF time."

"That sounds perfect."

The rest of the evening was more relaxed as Morgan and Jen spent most of the afternoon talking about boys, some shopping that they were planning for the next morning, and watching funny videos. Mrs. Neubauer, not one to really cook, ordered a couple delicious veggie pizzas, perfect sustenance for an extravagant Jen and Morgan photoshoot. After many wardrobe changes and poses—equal parts silly and sultry—Jen and Morgan had the perfect new Instagram picture: hands on hips, hair down, sunglasses on, and lips pursed. Their pose soon turned into a Tik Tok video that they checked religiously throughout the evening. After changing their profile pictures to their new fabulous BFF one, they proceeded to enthusiastically study a few profiles of boys they had crushes on, including Drake Furgerson and some of his soccer buddies, while simultaneously checking how many and who liked their new profile pics.

"Ya know, you girls would get all As if you studied your homework that thoroughly," Mrs. Neubauer added.

"Ha ha, Mom. Very funny, Jen already does get all As." Morgan replied.

"I got a B once," Jen replied with a giggle.

"I'm just trying to help her be more well-rounded," Morgan added with a smile.

"I'm not sure Jen needs to be rounded like that. Jen, maybe you can help round Morgan into getting straight As too," Mrs. Neubauer responded with a raised eyebrow.

"I'm sorry, I don't think anyone could help her." Jen giggled.

"Whatever! I get all As and Bs," Morgan said in laughing protest.

"Goodnight, girls. Have fun. Your dad is finishing up a college football game, and I'm going to go read. You can probably watch a movie when he's done. Don't stay up too late. We still have some shopping to do in the morning."

"Thank you so much Mrs. Neubauer for everything."

"Jen, I just want to tell you how proud I am of you. Just, just . . . ah . . . everything you go through, I . . . I just, am really proud of you."

"Thanks," Jen said, suddenly shy.

"Well goodnight, girls."

"Goodnight!" the girls said in unison.

The girls finished the night watching *Serendipity*, one of Mrs. Neubauer's and recently Morgan's old favorite movies.

As Jen and Morgan lay in Morgan's queen-size bed, Jen re-appreciated Morgan's cushy pillows and hot pink comforter. The night air wafted into the slightly ajar window giving the room that perfect warm but cool sleeping temperature.

"I think Drake Furgerson and I are lover-soulmates that are just one missing glove away from coming together," Morgan stated with a more breathy voice than usual.

"No way. Drake is my man! I'm going to bring a glove Monday morning to leave so he'll have to return it to me."

"I'll bring one first!"Morgan laughed.

The girls fell asleep, dreaming of providential and everlasting ninth grade love.

Chapter 4

Beeeep, beep beep beep. Beeeep, beep beep beep.

"Shut up!" Jen growled at the alarm clock app on her Ipod. Craving more sleep, she wished for a few extra minutes before her mom would be in to wake her. There were few things that annoyed Jen more fiercely than her mom in the morning. Lana bothered her so much that she started setting her alarm ten minutes before her mom was sure to come in. Jen preferred the loud robotic beeps to her mom's shrill voice.

On church mornings, Lana would come into Jen's room at exactly 7:30 a.m. on the dot. The thing that perplexed and irritated Jen most was that church didn't start till ten, and Sunday school didn't start till nine. Not to mention, they only lived five minutes away, and even with Lana's ten mph under-the-speed limit driving, it still only took them seven minutes to get there. Jen always secretly prided herself on not being one of those "girly girls" that took forever to get ready. She needed not a second over twenty minutes. She rarely ate breakfast, so according to her calculation, Lana got her up exactly one hour earlier than she needed to get up. It was especially brutal when she actually had something to do Saturday evening. As much as Jen tried to fight it, Lana refused to wake her up any later. She used to fight with her mom constantly about getting up but she had finally come to the realization that fighting with her mom to let her sleep in just woke her up more by the sheer effort it took to argue, and put her in a much more sour mood. It was a losing battle. The only solace she found was that if she woke up to the alarm, she was better able to bear her mom's high-pitched wake up call a few minutes later.

Church was a source of mixed feelings for Jen. She was pretty sure she believed in God and Jesus and all that, but didn't really like church that much. It annoyed her. Lana was adamant about their family attending church, almost militant about it. It was one of the not-optional things in their family. Sunday was church day. It wasn't that she was necessarily against church she just felt it was pointless. Church was full of people who talked about love and doing nice things, but in practice, it felt like a special club for lame, close-minded, and judgmental adults. It's not that the people were mean. They were friendly. Just don't cross them or get *caught* doing anything sinful.

Jen recalled what happened to eleventh grader Kim Kelly last summer after she was caught smoking a cigarette outside during a Sunday evening Bible study. She was practically excommunicated from the church. *I'm sure Kim would have wished for that,* Jen thought. Instead, Kim got to have a two-hour meeting with the pastor and her parents as they all told her to repent or she was going to hell. The whole 165 people that attended First Congregational Community Church either avoided her altogether or glared at her as if their laser stares could somehow zap the sinful uncleanness from her skin. Jen overheard one mom fiercely reprimand her kindergartener who she found throwing a ball with Kim a couple weeks later. "You are *not* to *ever* go near *her* again!" Jen wondered if the mom thought that tobacco use was one of the most communicable and deadly diseases of the world and the thrown ball was the most common means of contamination, or if Kim had just been busted for an underground kindergarten tobacco ring that used the church as its headquarters.

Although there were a lot of things Jen hated about church, there was something soothing, almost peaceful when the morning sunlight would hit the emerald green, gold and blue stained glass windows at certain angles as they sang some of the prettier hymns. It was quite serene and made Jen think there might really be a God up there after all, but those moments were few and far between. Most moments were spent thinking about how annoying the people at her church were.

"Come on, Jennifer. It's almost time to go."

"I've been sitting here for thirty minutes, Mom, just like every week," Jen replied, slightly annoyed by her mom's useless declaration.

"Ronnie, how many times have I told you not to play video games before church."

"Mom, it's fine! I'm already ready," Ronnie shouted back.

"Is that the same shirt you had on yesterday? Go change now, Ronnie. We're going to be late. And comb your hair. It's almost time to go."

"Right after I beat this guy," Ronnie protested.

"Do you want to be grounded from video games?" Lana slightly raised her voice in reply.

"Okay, okay! I've already beat that guy before." Ronnie sprinted to his room.

"I'm glad Ronnie gets to do whatever he wants and doesn't get grounded," Jen added, staring at her mom wondering where she got yellowish eyeshadow to match her yellow blouse. Jen thought it made Lana's eyes look like dual sunsets.

"Jen, you know that's not true. Ronnie, you are *not* wearing that to church! With that awful skateboarder guy on your shirt! This is *church*, Ronnie! Not the playground!"

"What!? It's fine, Mom!"

"Ronnie, get back there and put on church clothes!"

"Okay!"

"We're going to be late!"

The Morris family was not late. They took their seats fifth row back, right side. Same as they had sat for the last twelve years. Jen often thought that the imprints of their backsides were probably indented into the velvet mauve-colored pew cushions. No matter what day or how many people were in attendance, the Morris family never moved more than three feet in either direction, even to accommodate the influx of people on Christmas or Easter. They always viewed the church service from this spot.

Ten-year-old Ronnie went to the children's service. Jen was jealous of the current state of the children's service, which from

Jen's observations, now consisted of watching <u>Veggie Tales</u> and eating candy. *When I was in kid's service, we just sat still and listened to lectures of how we should obey our parents taken from the King James Bible.*

Reverend Robert Scott Shepherd took the podium after a few First Congregational Community Church staple hymns. Reverend Shepherd was a nice enough person. His partly grey hair was perfectly combed to the side in a puffy fashion. His black suits held white shirts and his white shirts held muted, solid-colored ties always held perfectly straight by a gold cross-shaped tie-tack, and continuing down to the top of his belt. He seemed to have an obsession with orderliness. There were many occasions where he would walk quietly over to a stack of papers or hymnals or curtains and straighten them up in the middle of a hymn. He walked quietly enough, trying not to distract from the song; however, it was hard not to notice someone moving among a crowd of still and pious people. Sometimes the organist, Mrs. Wallace, would notice Reverend Shepherd slowly walking across the platform and picking up a stray piece of paper. She would look annoyed, although she would never dare say anything to him. Jen found Reverend Shepherd to be friendly in person but difficult in conversation. He was a little socially awkward and would say "hello" and "how are you?" but would usually wait until someone spoke to him to say something further.

Jen tended to be apprehensive in his presence, although Reverend Shepherd really was a kind person. God, Himself, only knew how many times Reverend Shepherd had helped out their family over the years, but when it came to actually talking to him, she felt as if she were always stepping barefoot around the broken glass of unspiritual conversation topics.

Jen vividly remembered a conversation they'd had a year ago. Jen had been trying to get her mom to head to the car after Sunday morning service (a weekly occurrence), but Lana, socialite in training, would talk at length to any person who would listen to her. After talking to Reverend Shepherd for almost ten minutes, Lana turned to talk to Mrs. Wallace to lobby for her favorite hymns the following week, leaving Jen and Reverend Shepherd to stand next to each other and exchange pleasantries. It seemed to Jen that Reverend Shepherd was only filling the duties of courtesy, but had little actual interest in what Jen thought. Jen replied to Reverend Shepherd's indifferent question of "How was your weekend?" and "What did you do?" and casually told him that she and her cousin Mario from Michigan watched one of the Star Wars movies the day before. Immediately his attention perked, and he quickly became interested and then began a lecturing rant about how Star Wars seems innocent but it really was based on Buddhist principles and how it was really evil or something. Jen, frozen in shock, barely heard the rest of what he had said because she was so embarrassed. Reverend Robert Scott Shepherd soon after told Lana his thoughts and Jen has since been sentenced to a lifetime apart from Star Wars, at least under Lana's watch. Jen felt 'the force' was not with her.

Reverend Shepherd began the morning service: "Good morning congregation. This morning I am blessed by God to make a special announcement. We the people of the First Congregational Community Church are honored to have a new youth minister that will be coming to our church. Reverend Adam Jenkins and his wife Lindsey are coming to our church from Michigan. They were youth ministers at a church in Michigan and are coming to our fellowship to help with the young people here at First Congregational Community Church. They are excellent people. We know Adam and Lindsey very well. Lindsey is actually Donna's second cousin."

Lana let out a quiet gasp, followed by "Jen!" in a voice that was half whisper and half squeak. She patted Jen's leg annoyingly and smiled. Jen countered with a roll of her eyes, a shake of her head and a slight shudder of her torso. Jen was not impressed.

Jen was forced on three occasions to attend young people's events at her church. She remembered each one clearly. Each one was more boring than the last, even painfully so. She wasn't beaten and tortured physically, just mentally. The few "events" or "unevents," as Jen thought was the more appropriate term, were the most boring events of her life. Jen remembered sitting in a classroom hearing lectures about sin, then listening to crappy Christian pop music while playing Scrabble for the "fun time." Usually, four to six kids attended the "unevents," and they were hosted by Mrs. Mary Browning. Mary Browning was the mother of Brian Browning, an introverted and awkward home-schooled high schooler. Mrs. Browning was convinced that her son needed more social interaction. Jen wouldn't disagree with this fact, unless, as in these youth events, the social interaction entailed Brian interacting with her. Jen could recall her mother's words verbatim.

"You are forced by church social obligation to attend these events."

Church social obligation? Seriously?!? What the heck is that?! And who the bleep cares about that?

Jen felt sure her mom was just regurgitating a statement made by Mrs. Browning. Lana always savored the moments when people invited her or her family to meet socially, as it was a rarity. Ultimately, Jen attended the unevent, which involved a forty minute lecture on the evils of secular music and played the world's all-time worst game of charades. The announcement of a youth minister probably meant more "unevents" for Jen to suffer through, and made Jen's mind begin to relive each one, until she began her imaginary rebuttal to Reverend Shepherd's announcement.

She pictured herself standing up and shouting:

"We have a youth minister coming to our church so we have to come to church even more?! Don't we come enough?! Just because your cousin needs a job I have to be tortured? Who would ever want to attend another young people event?! First, these "fun" events are hosted at church, and who could ever feel comfortable in church enough to actually attempt to have fun? And they are not fun! They are what old, lame, boring, and judgemental people think are fun. Not what young people could ever perceive as fun, outside of maybe, the few weird kids that do attend!"

Jen's thoughts shot straight to the aftermath of such a rebuttal and the hours of long meetings with the Reverend Shepherd and her mother and the inevitable church apology she would have to make. Jen shook her head and felt relieved she didn't make her protest, but still felt as if a dark cloud was suddenly floating over her.

Jen spent the rest of the day finishing her homework, watching TV, reading, telephoning Morgan, and doing whatever she could to not think about church.

Chapter 5

M r. Well's fifth period biology class went on for longer than
normal. Mr. Wells seemed to have the gift of boredom. If Jen's
mind could think past the mind-numbing monotone voice itself, it
was really almost humorous how boring he was.

Jen wondered, *is Mr. Wells trying to bore the class brain-dead?
How could he not be? Can anyone have that little self-awareness?
Isn't there a public speaking class teachers have to take somewhere
along the way to be teachers? How did Mr. Wells pass? Maybe Mr.
Wells, after years of teaching kids who gave him trouble, decided,
since corporal punishment has been banished in the public schools,
that the only way he could get back at the students was to purposely
and sadistically bore students till their brains were on the verge of
cerebral hemorrhaging, and that Mr. Wells was really a maniacal
evil genius, and that underneath his lavishly plain exterior and un-
canny monotony he was really laughing with all the hearty enthusiasm of one of the greatest of villains of all time! Wow.* Jen shook
her head. *I must be bored. People who are enjoying themselves in
class don't have such vivid daydreams of their teachers being evil
maniacal geniuses."*

*If only Morgan was in this class. Everything is always better
when Morgan is around. Together, Morgan and I could even survive
a class with Mr. Wells.* Jen accidentally let out an audible sigh, causing bored classmates to glance over to her.

Now all she could do was sit and stare at Drake Furgerson.
Drake Furgerson played soccer and was considered to be one of
the most popular kids in school even though he was only a freshman. He looked as if he walked out of a magazine. He was decently

tall with a muscular frame that made him seem older than fifteen. He was so beautiful, in a handsome way that it made Jen almost despise him. He had dirty blond hair that was flipped up in a stylish fashion and the most uniform and perfect face and skin. If it weren't for his sharp wit that made him stand out from the other popular kids, Jen probably wouldn't pay any attention to him at all. Jen rarely had a chance to talk to him directly. She and he did have a few "flirty little chats" (as Morgan called them) in class. Part of Jen wished they really were flirting, but she doubted that Drake had any interest in her. He had just about every pretty girl in the freshman class, and many in older grades constantly giggling about him and suggesting that they hang out on the weekends. Three weeks into the school year and already, there were always girls babbling on about him. 'Drake winked at me'. 'Drake's so dreamy'. 'Drake bumped into me'. 'Drake handed me a plastic fork . . .'

Lame. Those girls need to get a life. At least when I talk to him, I know that he's really not in love with me.

It was just last period that Jen overheard two of the more loquacious girls in her class talking about how Haylee Roberts, a junior and popular girl extraordinaire, was going to take Drake to homecoming which would have been the first time a freshman boy had gone with an upperclassman girl in school history or something blah blah blah. *It's all nonsense,* Jen thought. Yet she could see what Haylee Roberts saw in him. There was something about him that made him seem different. It wasn't that he wasn't shallow. He was, but he was also intelligent, funny, very confident and quick on his feet. And his occasional deep thoughts and insights in class, however fabricated they might be, made his teachers think highly of him, and helped Jen think that maybe there was something deeper than his Abercrombie model exterior.

Class was almost over. Mr. Wells was almost finished talking. Jen wasn't sure she caught anything that he said. As she glanced around the room it was clear that no one else was listening either. *Mr. Wells probably doesn't even know what he's saying. He's probably been daydreaming of some scientist woman he met at the last biology teacher's conference who wore thicker glasses than he did. Yuck!*

Ugh, why am I thinking about Mr. Well's romantic life!? Yuck. I must be bored! Okay, four minutes left! Okay, he's finally finishing. Phew! That was painful.

Mr. Wells finished with assigning the next chapter in their biology book. Jen read the biology chapters religiously in order to catch up with what she would inevitably miss in the lectures. As Mr. Wells returned to his desk and students began to talk among themselves, Drake who usually sat exactly two rows over and two seats up from Jen, (not that Jen ever noticed) came and sat directly in front of her to talk to Seth Wade a carefree middle defender from the soccer team who sat in the next row. Jen couldn't help but listen and pretend not to be listening, while she nonchalantly began running her fingers through her hair fixing any strays.

"Seth, could you believe how much Coach made us run yesterday?"

"That was bull s——!"

"Yeah we weren't even the ones that made those penalties. We're punished 'cause Marcus and Corie can't play soccer."

"I know! Right? BS."

"Hey Jen, did you get that English reading done?" Jen was startled by Drake suddenly addressing her.

"Wait, what? Oh the English assignment . . . ummm . . . yeah I finished it," Jen answered in an oddly breathy manner that slowly faded into her normal voice, after she noticed how strangely she was talking.

"What was the story about? I didn't get to read it. We had a crazy soccer practice last night."

"Yeah . . . it was uh . . . It was just about this old guy who imagined himself doing all these exciting things, though in reality, he was really old and had to have his wife help him with everything. It was okay."

"So he just imagined himself doing all these things?"

"Yeah. He imagined himself like he was this superhero or something, but could like barely walk in real life."

"Okay. Thanks Jen! I heard we're going to have a quiz."

As he quickly and casually rested his hand on hers for a second he looked right at her smiling and said: "You're a lifesaver," before turning back to Seth as the bell rang.

This sent Jen's mind whirling, while a smile broke out across her face and butterflies took flight in her stomach.

What did he mean by touching my hand? Does he like me? Jen, it's Drake Furgerson. Every girl in the school wants him. He's not going to pick you. He did just touch my hand, though! I don't think he meant anything by it but it really felt nice. I couldn't even imagine having him as my BAE! Every girl in the school would be so jealous. You're getting ahead of yourself, Jen. He touched your hand, he didn't take it in marriage.

Chapter 6

"Attention all Hemlock Ridge High School students, there will be mandatory tryouts next Tuesday after school for all who are interested in being part of the fall play called 'Identities.' Please see the new theater teacher Ms. Collins for any additional details."

"Can you believe they are finally doing play tryouts?" Jazmine said, interrupting the remaining end-of-day announcements.

"Yeah they were supposed to be two weeks ago," Jen answered in a hush tone.

Mr. Freeman looking over, "Girls no talking during announcements! Geez, I don't know how many times I have to say it. I must have said it 200 times this year and we're only in the fourth week of school, always without a doubt there has to be someone talking!"

"Sorry . . . " Jen said quietly.

"I'm sorry, Mr. Freeman," Jazmine replied with a smile.

"It's fine. I just get pretty sick of talking about it," Mr. Freeman answered in a less upset tone.

"Have you lost weight Mr. Freeman? You look thinner than you did at the first week of school," Jazmine added again with her brilliant smile.

"Well, yes, I have been working out, I could be a little thinner than I was a few weeks ago, I did get this new shirt," responded Mr. Freemen flattered that someone noticed the not so flattering, tighter than it should be, black, athletic cut polo.

"Looks nice Mr. Freeman," Jazmine said with a voice that oozed flattery. The class began talking as well, taking note that Mr.

Freeman was no longer paying attention to the announcements and was himself talking during the announcements about his own diet and exercise plan.

Jazmine whispered to Jen while still looking at Mr. Freeman smiling and nodding her head, "I learned from my older brothers that if you can get a teacher talking about themselves they usually will become so distracted that they'll waste huge portions of class . I usually only try to get them talking during boring lectures but I really didn't want to listen to the stupid Friday afternoon announcements with only ten minutes left."

"That's so funny," Jen said with a laugh. "Don't the teachers ever catch on?"

"No not usually. Most just like talking about themselves so much they don't even notice. The only problem comes when the teachers' talking about themselves becomes more boring than the subject you're trying to avoid learning. So there's definitely risk involved."

"That's so funny," Jen answered again with a laugh.

Another very slender ninth grade boy began asking Mr. Freeman some questions about working out, releasing Jazmine from her fake listening act.

"So are you going to the freshman football game on Saturday? You know my boyfriend Sean is playing right? Varsity plays on Fridays and freshman on Saturday. You should come!"

"Well, I would but I got this thing at our church. I really don't want to go but I know my mom will make me go."

"Oh, really? Well that's okay, but you really should come out sometime. Nobody goes to the freshman games on Saturday. The freshman team is actually pretty good too, and our varsity team sucks. They only won like two games last year."

"Yeah, I heard that. At least our school soccer team is good, right?"

"Yeah our soccer team was like third in state last year. And our football team was like third worst or something. And man, some of those soccer boys are cute too! If Sean and I ever break up, that'll be the first thing I do; join the soccer team."

"Don't they have a girl's team?"

"Yeah, but I'd join the boys team. All those practices, long bus trips, and group showers!"

"Jazmine!" Jen said with a shocked laugh.

"What?! Just sayin'," Jazmine said with a smile.

The bell rang and Jen ran to her locker to grab her biology book before going out to the bus. The bus driver did not mess around when it came to punctuality. Betty had the bus ready to move the second it was time to leave. Students learned very quickly that they were either on time or left behind. Students who had ridden with Betty before knew this and took it seriously while new students often were left behind a couple times before they realized Betty's strict adherence to the bus schedule.

At the end of school, Jen always felt like she was going to get run over or hit. Sometimes she felt like she was in a giant football game and everyone was trying to knock her over. Jen remembered what her cousin Mario from Michigan once told her. Mario was obsessed with football. He was actually a big Cleveland Browns fan, despite being from Michigan. Mario believed being a Cleveland Browns fan had made him a better person because it forced him to deal with defeat and failed expectations. She remembered specifically what Mario once said about the crowded hallways in his school: "Sometimes when I'm in a rush in the hallway I pretend that I'm a running back looking for my opening and that the people in front of me are my lead blockers, and I'm looking for that crease so I can take it to the house." Jen wasn't sure about all that; mostly because she wasn't completely sure what that meant but she felt like she got hit enough in the hallway that she could be in a football game. *At least in a real football game, you have helmets and pads and you know you're going to get hit.*

The crowded halls Jen usually avoided had delayed her just enough to only barely get to the bus before it left. As Jen looked at her watch, her pace quickened. One minute until Betty took off. Jen was now in sight of the bus and could see Betty glance at her watch and reach for the door lever. Jen yelled to her "Wait!" Betty saw Jen and shook her head. She grumpily said, "Come on! I'm leaving!" Jen skipped a step, hopping onto the bus and searched for an empty seat. Arriving to the bus later than expected, Jen found the selection of seats to be wanting. All of Jen's usual seats in the front were occupied, leaving only a few seats toward the back. Jen dropped her belongings into the frontmost of the back seats, leaving only one empty seat between her and the normal "bus ruffians." "Bus ruffians" was the term Morgan gave for the weird, "think they're cool" kids who sat in the back of the bus. The name was an homage to the odd term Lana liked to use for anyone she considered unruly.

As Jen slouched back against the green vinyl seat, one of the boys took notice that Jen was actually sitting toward the back of the bus and said: " Hey Jen I'm glad you finally came and sat by us."

Jen answered with a nod of the head and a forced half chuckle.

"She thinks she's too cool to sit with us," said one of the ruffians.

"Yeah I'm not sure why she thinks she's so cool. Her mom is like retarded or something," added an overweight kid named Frankie in a loud mocking tone.

"She is not retarded!" Jen answered, turning towards the back of the bus and almost shouting. Immediately Jen realized that she had spoken to them and that they would now only bother her more. Frustrated that she didn't think and just reacted, Jen faced forward, closed her eyes for a moment, and shook her head knowing she shouldn't have said anything at all.

"Woah, well, look who finally spoke up," said a kid named Jake.

"She's probably just upset because she's retarded too. Ya know it's genetic," added Chance trying to impress his friends.

"No, she gets like straight As or something, so she's probably adopted."

"Talk about bad luck, getting adopted by a retarded woman."

At this, Jen violently grabbed her belongings and strode up the center aisle to a recently vacated seat two rows up with a tear dripping from her eye. Betty glanced in her mirror and saw Jen move out of her seat and yelled:

"Sit down! There is no moving on the bus!"

Jen's single tear dripping down her face was spotted by Ronnie sitting a couple seats up and across.

"What happened Jen? Are you okay?" Ronnie asked from across the bus looking very concerned to see his usually strong sister upset.

"I'm fine."

"Jen what happened?!"

"I'm fine. Leave me alone!"

Ronnie looked toward the back of the bus, hearing the ruffians explode with laughter.

"Jen what happened?" Ronnie asked with a lowered vocal tone.

"I'm fine. Leave me alone!" Jen yelled in a tone that drew the attention of the passengers in the five nearest seats.

Jen stared out the window, watching more houses and trees go by, waiting for the final moments when she could leave this awful ride home. Jen knew that the boys in the back were jerks. A group that despite being either overweight, homely looking or unintelligent, felt their duty to try and make fun of others as much as they most likely had been ridiculed themselves. Jen knew that, but had a bigger fear that these boys that had rode the bus with Jen for years and knew her family and its dysfunctions would tell other people about her family. How long would it be before her other high school classmates learned of her mom? Jen didn't want to think about it, but sometimes the things that Jen wanted to think about the least were the things she thought about the most. Part of Jen felt bad that she was embarrassed at all about her family. Her mom had problems; so what? Lots of families have problems, but the reality was that her mom constantly did do embarrassing things. Jen's mind continued to wander.

Next time I have to sit in the back, I'm going to walk home even if it is a blizzard outside. At least I don't have class with any of those idiots. I don't need any of my actual intelligent classmates teasing me. I just want to go spend time with Morgan. She makes everything better. Have some nice Morgan time, and not think about obnoxious people. *Seriously Morgan would punch these kids in the face. She does not play. She would cuss them out till they cried and only stop to throw some more punches.*

The mental visualization of Morgan punching and cussing out the boys in the back of the bus made Jen feel much better, and she even cracked a smile. The bus pulled up to the Morris residence and Jen practically sprinted off the bus but still heard some muffled laughing and the word "retard" coming from the back of the bus. Ronnie followed Jen, walking as quickly as he could until a jog was necessary to catch up to Jen.

"Jen, they were calling mom retarded weren't they," he said, trying to catch his breath.

"Yeah, they were. Don't worry about it. They're just a bunch of idiots."

"The kids at my school used to say stuff like that until Ms. Kennett found out and said it was bullying and the kids got in really big trouble. Nobody really says anything anymore."

"That's good . . . that they stopped . . . " Jen's sentence trailed off as her and Ronnie froze when they finally saw Lana kneeling on the other side of the car holding some stray weeds while sporting her gardening apparel.

"My babies! How are you? That's good that they stopped what?" Lana asked getting up from her knees so she could hug her children. Jen and Ronnie looked surprised and Jen quickly but suspiciously finished her sentence.

"That's good they don't . . . *watch those bad movies anymore.*"
Ronnie gave her a look like *Really? Bad movies?*

"Yeah it's good," he responded, not sounding very convinced.

"You're friends aren't watching bad movies again, are they?" Lana asked, sounding very concerned, while wrapping her arms around Ronnie. "It's not Robbie Sutton again is it?"

"No mom. Jen is just talking about some other friends."

"Okay, but you know I don't want you hanging out with kids that are watching bad movies."

"I know, Mom."

"How was school, Jen?" Lana asked, now moving over to hug her.

"Good, Mom."

"How are your grades?"

"Good," Jen said through a hug that was more intense than she expected.

"You're in high school now and it gets a lot harder. You have to really study. Are you studying enough, Jen?"

"Yes, Mom! I'm studying enough," Jen said as she finally broke free of the hug.

"Okay, well you need to study Jen. High school is much harder than grade school. You really have to study."

"Yeah I got it, Mom. Do you know where the phone is so I can call Morgan."

"Are you sure you shouldn't spend some time studying instead?"

"Mom, geez how many times do I have to tell you?! I'm fine. I'm all studied up. I said that like four times."

"I'm sorry, Jen. You know I worry sometimes. I just had a hard time in high school. I had to study much more than you do. But I know I have a harder time with things than you do."

Jen started to feel bad for being so impatient with her mom.

"No, it's okay, Mom. I'm just fine. I only have a few classes with tests coming up and I have As and Bs in all of my classes, and I think the Bs are pretty close to being As. I just have to see how I did on the last few homework assignments. So I'm fine, Mom."

"I'm so proud of you, Jenny!" Lana said with a giggle.

"Thanks, Mom. Do you know where the phone is? I just want to call Morgan real quick. She wasn't at history class today."

" I don't know, Jenny. I think it might be on the kitchen table."

Looking for the phone annoyed Jen again. Her family was the only family she knew of that had a landline. When she finally found the white cordless phone, Jen called Morgan, but she was on the phone with Zoey Davidson, another freshman who just transferred in from Florida. Morgan explained that her and Zoey were going to the football game and that she was welcome to come with them if she wanted. Jen was a little disappointed that Morgan wasn't free to spend bff time with her. Jen knew Lana wouldn't have the eight dollars it took for students to go to the football game and she had spent her money on new school clothes. She hoped that Morgan would offer to pay her way into the game as she had done many times before, but Morgan made no such offer and Jen felt bad bringing it up. Her heart sank. Jen tried her best not to sound too upset as she hung up quickly but was unsure if her attempt to sound chill actually worked. Jen sat there staring at the wall for a moment. It was only one night, but this was supposed to be her night to help rejuvenate her spirits but instead it turned to loneliness and boredom. Jen spent the rest of the night watching reruns of *The Vampire Diaries* and *Arrow* and using her neighbor's Wi-Fi to check social media to find what seemed like a record number of selfies from other freshmen having a good time at the football game. Jen went to sleep wondering what she would have looked like tagged in those photos.

Chapter 7

The first youth meeting was something Jen had been dreading for weeks. Lana, however, was ecstatic. Although it was supposed to be just an introduction, Lana had been reminding Jen every day. Reverend Adam Jenkins was going to be introduced to the church on Sunday. Apparently, Reverend Jenkins had requested a special Saturday meet-and-greet so he could meet the few middle and high school students in the congregation.

Jen searched through her closet for an outfit that would be stylish but not too stylish, since it was church. On the other hand, she could not dress too casually because it was church and Lana never let Jen leave the house in anything that wasn't "church appropriate," a category which Lana defined much differently than Jen did. Jen's own style leaned much more casually than her mom's. Lana loved sequins and lace and even managed to get them on sweatshirts, sweaters, and polos. "T-shirts are for bedtime," Lana would often say. Jen considered herself a T-shirt and jeans type girl. Apparel clashes abounded. "Give me a comfy tee and a slightly loose fitting pair of jeans and I'll be happy," Jen would tell her best friend Morgan.

Despite pretty facial features and a medium build that was thin but curvy, Jen believed herself to be plain. She felt she had "boring straight hair" and eyes that her and her friend Jessica endearingly referred to as "poop-colored." Morgan often told Jen that with a little confidence she would be one of the prettiest girls in school. Jen often thought Morgan was full of it. Morgan did make Jen feel more confident at least when Jen wasn't comparing herself with her. Morgan was so fashionable and had model-like perfection to her features despite being a little short. Jen, comparatively, was taller, had slightly broader shoulders and lacked the fashion sense of a Neubauer but was nonetheless prettier than she realized.

Jen wanted Morgan to come meet the youth minister with her but she knew that after all the venting and complaining she did about church, especially the couple young people's outings she had gone to, Jen knew there was no way Morgan would go.

Lana and Jen pulled into the mostly paved parking lot of the church at quarter to six. Jen looked at her watch and rolled her eyes seeing that they were fifteen minutes early even to this. She knew she would have to wait in the fellowship hall with her mom who was annoyingly over-excited.

Lana confirmed her obvious excitement in the parking lot by admitting with a big smile and a voice that squeaked to keep constraint: "I am so excited!"

"I'm glad *you're* excited!"

"I am!" Lana said oblivious to her daughter's lack of enthusiasm.

"I need to use the restroom. I'll meet you down there," Jen said, glad she'd thought of an excuse to just be alone for a minute.

"Okay, but hurry up Jenny. You don't want to miss anything."

She did need to use the restroom but even more so needed a minute to gain the mental-emotional stability necessary to withstand the next thirty minutes. Jen stood by the gaudy brass mirror surrounded by mauve wallpaper of roses. She stared, wondering why her church needed a young people's minister to bore the students more individually and more frequently. At least with the Sunday morning church service, it was only an hour once a week and Jen could do her time, remain somewhat anonymous, and be done with it for the week. To be in a small group with those couple weird and irritatingly boring kids was more than she could handle, especially when some church prison guard armed with judgmentalness was monitoring her every move. Jen knew that her alone time was quickly running out, and she had to face the music sooner than later. As she turned the corner to the exit she saw in the thin glass that ran beside the bathroom door Reverend Shepherd talking to a young Asian-looking man. The man was thinly muscular and medium in height and build. He had spiky hair, wore a youthful rugby-style short sleeve polo- white with aqua stripes, jeans light in color with a slight rip in the left knee and a necklace that looked like it was made of shells. He could pass for Hawaiian but Jen was not sure. Jen froze to listen in on them, not wanting to go out there and have to talk to Reverend Shepherd or the young man.

"Is that what you're wearing?" Reverend Shepherd asked in a lowered voice that seethed disappointment. The young man looked a little embarrassed or annoyed Jen couldn't quite tell.

"Yeah I didn't think this would be that formal," he said, rocking back on his heels.

"No, I'm sorry it's my fault. It's fine," Reverend Shepherd said shaking his head. "Well, my computer is this way. I'm not sure if I have a virus or what but I haven't been able to check my email for a week."

"Yeah, let's take a look," the man responded positively as the two began walking up the maroon carpeted ramp towards Reverend Shepherd's office.

Jen sighed audibly. *It's just like Reverend Shepherd to give the computer tech support guy a lecture on dress code before he lets him fix his computer. Not everyone wears long sleeved white dress shirts everyday of the year, Reverend Shepherd.*

Jen walked down to the fellowship gathering room. She took a seat next to her mom, happy that her little brother was at a friend's house. Jen glanced around to see two of the other young people, Brian Browning and his mom, and his cousin Emma and her mom. Jen cringed in annoyance. Brian's cousin, Emma, had been to two other gatherings and Jen could barely stand her. Jen hunched over and put her face in her hands and stared at the floor in boredom as her mom exchanged pleasantries with Mrs. Browning. A few seconds later as Jen was still staring at the floor, Jen caught sight of a pair of white with blue striped Pumas and the light wash jeans come into the room next to the black loafers and black dress pants. As her eyes panned up and saw the young Asian computer tech support guy next to Reverend Shepherd, Jen wished they could just fix the stupid computers so they could get the tortuous meeting over with.

"Eh hem," Reverend Shepherd cleared his throat loudly. "Welcome and thank you for coming. Without further ado, I would like to introduce the new youth minister of First Congregational Community Church, Mr. Adam Jenkins."

It had been a while since Jen had actually heard audible gasps, but she heard several the moment Reverend Shepherd announced the new youth minister. She and Brian were the only ones to not give a gasp at the surprise announcement. Brian, glanced up, for a partial moment, and then went back to staring at the floor as he had done before. Jen thought he probably went back to thinking about his World of Warcraft game he was obsessed with. Jen made no gasp but her eyes were very wide and her mouth slightly opened. She felt like Reverend Shepherd was telling a joke, yet she knew he did not have humor. She just kept staring in wonderment and surprise. She, of course, had no problem with Asian people or younger cool-looking people, she just was so shocked that the *church* was okay with that. Her church wasn't necessarily racist or prejudiced, but it was so racially and culturally monochromatic, that it was almost shocking that they had hired someone different. The other part that was somewhat shocking was this young Asian guy was pretty chic and cool looking which Jen felt was so odd for First Congregational Community Church. Almost all the people that went there had the most traditional and vanilla way of dressing, that it seemed so out of place to see someone who looked like they could play on "Hawaii 5-0" be a part of their church staff. Even if the church had decided to hire an Asian youth minister, Jen expected him to be a Reverend Shepherd clone, complete with black dress pants, white shirt, loafers, and the signature puffy hair combed to the side.

"Well, it's nice to meet all of you. Like Reverend Shepherd said, I'm Adam Jenkins. I'm from Michigan. I was a youth minister at another church in Michigan, but I came here to this church, after talking to Reverend Shepherd and feeling like God was drawing us here to this community. This is a little bit different than the church I've been used to, but I'm excited for what God has in store for us at First Congregational Community Church."

"Does anyone have any questions for Reverend Adam?" added Reverend Shepherd.

Silence filled the room, as the six people in attendance tried to think of any questions. Judging by her mom's intense expression, it was obvious to Jen that Lana wanted to ask something but couldn't think of anything. After an uncomfortable minute Reverend Shepherd began, "I know there were a few people who couldn't make it to the meeting today. We will introduce Reverend Jenkins again on Sunday morning. Well if there are no questions . . . "

"Wait . . . what . . . is God . . . good?" the room stared in puzzlement as they attempted to understand what Lana was trying to say.

"I mean, what is good God give you? . . . I mean, what is something good God has blessed you with?"

"Um, okay," Reverend Adam answered with a smile. "Yeah well one of the biggest blessings in my life that I haven't yet mentioned is my wife Lindsey. She wasn't able to make it tonight, but she is the most incredible blessing I've ever had. She brings me joy everyday. We drive each other crazy sometimes but I wouldn't have it any other way. Another wonderful blessing is my family growing up. I was adopted by my family in Michigan. I am actually Korean. I never met my real parents, but the Jenkins family raised me and took care of me and loved me as their own, since I was very young. I am forever thankful to God and to them for that. Well, are there any other questions or . . . I would love to hear about you guys or tell me about yourselves, I feel like I'm rambling."

"Yes, hi, this is Mrs. Mary Browning, Brian's mom. I would like to know when you plan on having youth events and I was wondering specifically if you would be able to have a formal homecoming or prom dance for the students?"

The entire room, including her son Brian, Reverend Adam, and Reverend Shepherd, stared at Mrs. Browning with an identical look that could be best described as "Are you serious?" Only Lana stared wide-eyed because she thought it was a *good* idea.

Reverend Adam actually began to laugh until he realized that she *was* being serious. He restrained his laugh into a somewhat straight face, as fast and as best he could, once he figured out that she did not mean her question in jest.

"Ya know, I hadn't thought of that but I think that given this year, and homecoming season so close and all, I think that would be something we will have to skip this year, but could always discuss that for future years. We do plan on having youth meetings every Wednesday just for an hour or so from like seven to eight."

Mrs.Browning nodded in understanding, clearly disappointed but replied "That is true. To assemble a proper formal it would take months of planning and preparation."

Jen almost let out an audible sigh of relief about a church formal, but was not happy to hear about weekly meetings. Reverend Adam raised his eyebrows and looked right at Jen and smiled, seeming relieved as well. Jen returned his smile until she caught herself. She did not want her mom or Reverend Shepherd to see her smiling.

"Well, I'm excited to get to know you guys and will see you soon at our weekly services," Reverend Adam said with a smile. As Jen and Lana rose from their worn padded metal chairs, Lana took Jen by the arm to be first in line to talk to Reverend Adam as they grabbed the generic cookies and overly-sweet punch that were put out as refreshments.

"Hi Reverend Adam," Lana said, glowing. Reverend Adam simply smiled back, seemingly not weirded out by Lana's huge smile and focused gaze "Hi, what's your name?"

"Lana Morris. This is Jenny. She is so special." Jen couldn't help but roll her eyes and slightly shake her head. Reverend Adam gave a slight chuckle and said, "Hi Lana, and hello Jenny. You do, of course, seem very special." This time Jen offered a small gracious smile in return.

"Jenny, what school do you go to?"

"Hemlock Ridge."

"Oh, okay cool. I'm still getting to know the area but Hemlock Ridge is the local school? It's just right down the street, right?"

"Yeah."

"Okay cool, Jenny. I'm glad to meet you and excited to get to know you at upcoming youth meetings."

Jen half smiled as she was not excited about the upcoming youth meetings and answered with a half-hearted "Okay."

"Bye, Reverend Adam!" Lana said enthusiastically as they walked away.

"Bye Lana!" Reverend Adam said in matched enthusiasm, then turned to the next parent.

"I like him, Jenny," Lana said to Jen as they walked to the car.

"I know you do, Mom."

"He's such a handsome Chinese guy."

"Mom, he's not Chinese, he's Korean."

"Isn't Korea the same as China?"

"No, Mom, it's not. They don't even speak the same language. That'd be like calling you Mexican because America is by Mexico."

"We don't live by Mexico. We live in Ohio."

"Yes, Mom, but part of the United States is by Mexico, nevermind . . . but he's Korean not Chinese."

"Well whatever he is, he is handsome."

"*Mom!* You're so weird."

"What? He is."

"*Mom!*"

Chapter 8

Thursday's auditions were in the school's auditorium. Hemlock Ridge High School was built in the 1950s and was fortunate enough to have a full auditorium. Many newer area schools had multipurpose areas that were used for everything: theater, indoor soccer, pep rallies, mass food consumption, etc. Although the school was far from chic, with its dated black, white, and mint green color scheme and not always very clean interior, Jen thought it was nice to have a separate gym, cafeteria and auditorium. Jen's friend Britta went to Jefferson High School. Britta's school, which was much newer and nicer as a whole, had to utilize the same "open concept" space for the theater with rows of chairs that rolled in. While the chairs were nice, it was still the same place students ate lunch, complete with the sticky floors and awful acoustics for their production of *Guys and Dolls*. The only sound that annoyed Jen more than the acoustics was the noise from the sticky floor clinging to the soles of her shoes. As Jen was leaving she heard a parent complaining about the production's acoustics, and another quip, "Yeah, Luck had an echo tonight."

As Jen briskly walked to the hardwood door with the greenish-bronze patinated handle, she glanced in and saw a few students talking and laughing with Ms. Collins, the new theater department teacher. It was only a few minutes until tryouts, and there was no sign of Morgan. At first glance, Ms. Collins looked very young. If not for her business attire, she could pass for a high school student. Jen was a little jealous of the students who had study hall eighth period and were able to come to talk to the new theater teacher. A few of the more popular kids were already laughing and joking with Ms. Collins. It seemed a little unfair that they got to meet the theater teacher and make a good impression. Jen felt like an outsider since they were already all buddy-buddy with her. Jen was ready for Morgan to arrive so they could introduce themselves. Morgan was running late. Jen walked back up the slight grade of the auditorium aisle to the hallway to look for Morgan. Her eyes scanned the end-of-school crowd gathered near the glass enclosure separating the slightly newer part of the school building and the older original building. Jen finally caught Morgan talking to a thin but tall boy with sandy brown hair wearing a lime green T-shirt that said "Party Hard-YOLO." Jen smiled when she saw him. It was obvious he liked Morgan but he was trying to play it cool. Jen watched for a minute while the boy Morgan was talking to nodded his head slightly upward as if to show that he was cool stuff. After the boy left, Morgan stood there talking to Zoey Davidson. Jen glanced at her watch and saw it was almost time for the play tryouts to begin, and walked towards Morgan to tell her it was time for the audition.

"Morgan who was that?!" Jen said with an excited smile.

"Garrett Williams," Morgan said with a charmed expression.

"Oh hey, Zoey," Jen said, not wanting to be rude to Zoey.

Zoey looked up from her iPhone just long enough to say, "Hey," and nod before looking back down.

"But hey, Morgan, let's go. It's time for the play tryout. Are you ready?"

"Oh, I'm not going," Morgan said, giving a quick glance at Zoey.

"What? Why!?"

"Cause I don't want to be in the dumb school play."

"What!? Why?! Morgan, we always dreamt of being in high school musicals! You just said two weeks ago that you were excited for tryouts!"

"Well, Jen this isn't even a musical. It's some random weird play."

"Yeah, it looks seriously lame," Zoey added.

Jen started to give Zoey a dirty look until she caught herself.

"Uhm, yeah but if we're in this play it'll help ready ourselves for real musicals later this year or next year. The new drama teacher will know us and we'll have the inside track."

"Yeah, I just don't think I care about it that much," Morgan responded with a shrug. Jen looked at Morgan with a look equally perplexed and hurt. Morgan noticed the look and added she was sorry before Zoey changed the subject.

"Did Garrett text you yet?"

"No, not yet, but he is seriously cute."

"Yeah, and he's like best friends with Drake too."

"OMG he just texted me! He wants to know if we want to go to the movies tomorrow as a group."

"Yeah let's go. It'll be okay with your mom, right?"

"Yeah, she'll be totally fine," Morgan said with conviction. As her eyes glanced up from her phone, Morgan noticed Jen still standing there listening with a look of annoyance.

"Sorry, Jen, we gotta go. Maybe next play or next year."

"Okay, bye," Jen said a little more breathy than normal, as if she were sighing as she spoke.

"Bye," Morgan and Zoey both answered, still staring at their iPhone screens as they walked away.

It may have been jealousy of Morgan's new friend Zoey or the fact that Morgan and Jen had been planning on trying out for the high school play for years, and now, to use Morgan's term, she'd "flaked out" on Jen. Whatever the reason, instead of feeling depressed, she was just angry. Jen walked aggressively to the auditorium where it looked like Ms. Collins was starting to round people up to have a pre-audition meeting. Ms. Collins sat on the old but well lacquered wood stage so she was at a higher altitude than the students.

"Alright, students, I want to welcome you to the preliminary auditions of *Identities*, our school's fall production. I am Ms. Collins, the new theatrical production director of Hemlock Ridge High School. I will be supervising auditions and will be working with a committee to make final decisions on who will be a part of our fall production. I expect all auditionees to realize that although this is a high school play, I expect a certain amount of professionalism. Many of you may not be ready for that, so do not be surprised if you are not chosen for the play." Jen didn't think the way the young teacher fraternized with some of the older students really shouted professionalism.

"And with that, the auditions will begin. Freshmen first! Meet me over on stage left. All other students please wait in the audience seating." Jen's anger and drive to do well in the play tryouts quickly began to fade to anxiety.

Ms. Collins beckoned the group of freshmen around the front of the stage to the short stairs of what would be considered stage left. Ms. Collins carried a small navy colored notebook that had white polka dots and gold accents. She sat down near a triangular dent in the wood next to a bronze electrical outlet cover. Ms. Collins asked the students to sit in a circle on the floor with her.

"Okay. I will give you a line to say and I want you to read it with feeling."

"Just read the lines?" asked a girl with curly hair who was in Jen's ninth grade college prep English class.

"Yes, but with *feeling*," answered Ms. Collins in a way only a drama teacher could.

Ms. Collins passed out half sheets of paper at random. Jen glanced down at hers. It said, "They tell me everyone is important but sometimes I just don't feel like it. I feel like nothing. Sometimes, I just sit alone in my room and cry." Jen's eyes widened at the oddly depressing sentence. *This is what they want me to say? What kind of play is this?*

"Just read the lines on the paper. Each are lines from actual parts of the play. We'll start with the young lady on the left here. What is your name sweetie?" Ms. Collins said, pointing to the girl with the curly hair.

"Carrie."

"Okay, say your part, Carrie, with feeling!"

"Sometimes my life seems so hopeless I don't know where to turn!" Carrie said in a peppy and almost cheerful way, causing the eight other freshmen and Ms. Collins to stare with almost identically puzzled looks. Carrie smiled back, somehow not realizing the contradictory way in which she said her lines.

"Okay, thank you, Carrie. Okay next. Your name?" Ms. Collins said, turning to Jen. Jen was surprised that Ms. Collins had called on her despite the fact that Jen sat directly to the left of Carrie and they were going in a circle. Suddenly a nervous pain hit Jen's left side.

"Uhmmm . . . Jen."

"Okay, Jen say your line."

Jen hesitated, "They tell me everyone is important but sometimes I just don't feel like it. I feel like nothing. Sometimes, I just sit alone in my room and cry." She was so nervous, that her words fell out, each seemingly more uncertain than the last, till her voice almost shook by the last word. Jen sighed, and immediately wished that she could have said her line better.

"Brilliant! Absolutely brilliant! That was exactly how I envisioned this part being done. Great job, Jen! Jen, what's your last name?" Jen's eyes widened.

"Morris," Jen said with a little more confidence. Miss Adams jotted a quick note in her notebook.

"Class that is how you put feeling into a part! You have to feel the part, be the part, make love to the part until you are in perfect union with the part. Notice the emotion Jen put into the part. She made it seem like she really doesn't feel important. When you act, you need to convince your audience. She convinced us she doesn't feel important. Great job, Jen!"

Jen shook her head slightly and tried to hold back a slight smile both to Miss Collin's positive response to her reading and the copious amounts of enthusiasm in which she expressed her positivity. The irony was not lost on Jen that she was being praised for pretending to be unimportant when she really just felt unimportant with no pretension. Jen shook her head slightly and smiled again.

The rest of the students said their parts without much fanfare. Only the lines Jen and Carrie read were from the same character, the other students said their various parts with minimal reaction from Ms. Collins. Jen kept replaying what Ms.Collins had said in her head, still surprised at the serendipitous way she was able to say her lines. The tryouts ended and Jen left still trying to hide a smile.

Chapter 9

It was Friday and Morgan was going out with Zoey Davidson again. This time they were going to the movies to meet up with Morgan's new crush Garrett and his friends. Morgan almost sounded as if she wanted Jen to come, until she added that it was all Zoey's friends and that it was sort of a couples thing. Jen thought that wasn't really true since two of the sets of friends weren't actually together, although Morgan definitely wouldn't be opposed to being more than friends with Garrett. Jen didn't have the money to go to the movies, and she knew she really wasn't invited. Situations like this made Jen wonder what it would be like to be popular and never have problems with money. Boredom and depression followed. Jen found little relief from the melancholy she felt in her heart. It was as though everything good from her life was sucked out.

Morgan was one of the few bright spots in her life, and now Zoey seemed to have taken that away. Jen found it difficult not to despise Zoey. Zoey was the friend Jen always wanted to be to Morgan. Zoey was pretty, fun, and knew lots of boys. Zoey was more like Morgan than Jen was. Zoey always had money to go hang out. Zoey, complete with a working phone, could text Morgan in a moment's notice, whereas Morgan had to wait for Jen to be in the right spot in her house so her five year-old iPod touch could pick up the neighbor's Wi-Fi. Morgan could call Zoey and not have to make small talk with her annoying mom on a landline before conversing. Zoey could answer a Tik Tok, Instagram, or Snapchat message without waiting for her old, slow computer or iPod touch to load up. But most of all Jen felt that Zoey was so cool. Way cooler than she was. Zoey was a newer, prettier, updated version of Jen. As heartbreaking as it was, Jen decided that Zoey was probably a better friend to Morgan than she ever would be. What could she possibly offer Morgan? Maybe a half a lifetime of memories, at least since third grade? But this was high school now and no one wants to talk about how they peed in the pool when they were nine because they drank too much Kool-Aid.

Jen awoke Saturday morning, a little later than she'd intended. The alarm clock read 10:30. Lana usually would not let Jen sleep past 8:30 on the weekends, but with Lana working a Saturday at her job at the Williamstown Library, Jen's eyes got to rest a couple extra hours. Even with the extra rest, Jen felt exhausted. She woke up with a blah feeling. Jen couldn't decide if she felt empty, hurt, or just bored. Jen couldn't think of any specific reasons why she felt this way. Yes, there was Morgan and Zoey, the school play, and the fact that she did not have many friends, but those things usually didn't get her down this much. Jen stepped down placing her left foot directly onto Fifi's tail, which was lying, as Fifi was, next to Jen's bed. Fifi hissed and ran away.

"You're lucky it wasn't your face, ya stupid cat," Jen growled with extra half-awake grumpiness.

Jen opened the venetian blinds in her room. Still raining. Jen threw on her pink Old Navy flip flops and walked downstairs. She dragged her feet across the carpet, adding new accompaniment to the snapping of the pink polyfoam, smacking her heels with every step. Ronnie's video game was still much louder and could be heard from the stairs to the kitchen. Even more evidence of Ronnie's consciousness was the layer of granulated sugar on the counter between the glass sugar shaker with the blue metal top and the box of Lucky Charms cereal. Ronnie was the only person Jen had ever met that thought Lucky Charms didn't have enough sugar in it already. Ronnie would add extra sugar to Lucky Charms when Lana was gone. If she was present, Lana would never let Ronnie get away with that, something that Ronnie was well aware of.

"You're gonna rot your teeth out, Ronnie!"

"No I'm not."

"You better clean this crap up in here and brush your teeth or I'm telling Mom."

"I'll tell her you said the word 'crap.'"

"You just said the word too, just now. I'll tell her that you said it too."

"Nuh-uh! I only said it because you said it!"

"You still said it and I'll tell mom if you tell on me, *AND* I'll tell her about the cereal."

"Jen!"

"Seriously, Ronnie you need to clean this mess up before Mom gets here. Or I won't have to tell her, she'll see for herself. And brush your teeth!"

"Okay!"

Jen shook her head. Her mom was ridiculous about words like "crap," "sucks," and "shut up." If she only heard for a second how kids talked at school, she'd have a heart attack. Jen took her favorite "Ya Jamaican Me Crazy" mug, a gift from Aunt Julie's last vacation, out of the cupboard, added water, microwaved it for exactly two minutes, squeezed a little honey, and dropped a bag of tea. Lemon Zinger was the flavor of the day. She sat at the dining room table by the window, staring, sipping, watching the rainwater collect on a leaf of a small tree in the backyard. It filled, tipped, and emptied. Six to eight seconds was the cycle. Jen must have watched it ten times before she caught her reflection in the glass. She couldn't see any details of her face clearly, only the groups of shapes that outlined her head.

Why couldn't I be prettier? If I were prettier . . . boys would like me. If I were prettier I would make friends easier. If I were prettier, I would almost automatically be cooler. Popular boys would talk to me. Morgan would like me more. We would have things in common. We could talk about the boys that like us. No wonder Morgan likes Zoey more. Zoey's so pretty. Morgan has a lot more in common with Zoey than me.

Jen's eyes shifted back to the leaf. She sipped the hot sweet and sour tea holding it in her mouth for a moment, letting her tongue taste and feel every drop before swallowing.

Jen could not remember the last time she felt happy. Okay, if she really thought about it, it hadn't been that long, but Jen was not in the mood to remember that. Jen knew her life could always be worse, but there was a little bit of solace when she dove into the feelings and revelled in her sadness. She stared out at the puddles collecting in her worn, uneven, and broken asphalt driveway. Part of Jen wanted to go sit out in the rain and let the chilly drops wash the emptiness from her, but what happens if emptiness is washed away, she thought? What would replace it? More emptiness was the only thing Jen could think of. As she sat watching the rain, waiting for Lana to return with the Agatha Christie novel she promised to bring, the phone rang.

"Hello."

"Jen! Hey what's up?"

"Oh . . . hey Morgan," Jen answered surprised by Morgan's voice.

"Jen, you sound surprised to hear from me."

"Oh, yeah, uhm, well, no, yeah . . . "

"Jen, I know I've been spending a lot of time with Zoey, but we're still like best friends."

As encouraging as it was to hear from Morgan, part of Jen cringed when she heard the word "*like*" next to the term "best friends." A couple months ago that word "*like*" would have never been next to the words "best friends." Jen knew she was just being overly critical, but she couldn't help but dwell on that word longer than she should have in the middle of a conversation. When Jen didn't respond, Morgan said, "Jen. Jen. Hello."

Okay Jen, don't let on to the fact that you're upset.

"Yeah, we are. Who else would put up with your BS?" Jen said in a tone that was sufficiently sassy. Jen was proud of her good cover.

"Ha, yeah, you've probably put up with more than the average person. But I've had to put up with your intolerable taste in boys. Philip James anyone? And have you seen the way you pour a cup of tea? Where can a girl find proper service these days?" Morgan said switching to her best English accent to refer to the infamous tea pouring debacle involving a "proper" *Pride and Prejudice*-inspired Jen and Morgan sixth grade tea party and a distracted Jen missing the tea cup completely and pouring hot tea directly into Morgan's lap. Jen laughed so hard she snorted, causing Morgan to quip,

"Did you just snort? OMG. Who does that?"

"Ha. Okay, Morgan. You're usually the one that snorts!"

"I don't know what you're talking about," Morgan answered with fake assurance.

Still laughing, Jen said, "And Philip James? Ew! I said he looked cute one time when I saw him from behind wearing a baseball cap! I could barely see his face."

"Jen, don't deny your true love."

"Okay, whatever. Morgaaaaan!!! I miss you. We need to hang out soon."

"Yeah we should."

"How about tonight?"

"I can't, sorry. I promised Zoey that I'd go hang out with her at the mall. Her mom is trying to fix her up with some kid. He's like the kid of one of her mom's friends. I would kill my mom if she ever tried to fix me up with someone. Yeah so I promised I'd be there to make sure he wasn't a total creeper."

"Yeah, that's cool. I understand," Jen said trying to sound cool with it. She then added, "Hey, what happened with you guys going to the movies with Garrett and his friends?

"Oh, Garrett's friend got in trouble for smoking weed so they bailed on us. It was lame, so Zoey and I just hung out."

"Crazy," Jen responded, suddenly, feeling distant to Morgan.

"Definitely! Okay, shoot! Jen I gotta go, it's Zoey. I gotta see where we're meeting tonight. I'll call you right back."

Morgan called back ten minutes later and talked for a few more minutes. Although Morgan wasn't able to hang out with Jen, it was nice to catch up with her. Jen had finally gotten the chance to tell Morgan about her seemingly successful audition. Morgan started chanting, "Jenny! Jenny! Jenny!" Jen smiled over the phone. It felt so nice to know that someone cared and was proud of her. Jen would find out if she made the play the next day. Reluctant to make a big deal of it, she hadn't told Lana yet. However, after her conversation with Morgan and how genuinely nice it felt to have someone proud of her, she decided to tell her mom about her possibly good news.

Upon hearing the news Lana burst into tears, hugged Jen, and kept repeating "I'm so proud of you, Jenny. I'm so proud of you, Jenny. I never could have done anything like that. I'm so proud of you." Jen smiled.

Chapter 10

J en was not smiling. Wednesday had been draining. It made Jen want to do nothing more than to take a nap and not talk to anyone. It had been ten days since Jen had enjoyed cheers from her Mom and Morgan for her good audition, and now she wanted to quit. Though it was an accomplishment to get the part of "Low Self-Esteem Girl 2" in the play, as she found out officially the previous Monday afternoon, the first walk-through was a trainwreck. Although Jen had memorized her few short lines, it was the execution of said lines that was the problem. The stage directions for "Low Self-Esteem Girl 2" suggested the lines should be read without confidence. Jen practiced her lines over the phone with Britta who had been part of the theater program at Jefferson High School. She said Jen naturally nailed the lack of confidence. Britta had laughed so hard and told Jen that she was born for the part. However, Britta's only concern was that Jen said her lines too quietly, and that on stage Jen would have to speak much louder.

During today's first walk-through practice, Jen had been sick-to-her-stomach nervous about saying her lines in front of the other students. There were only a few freshmen in the play and an abnormal amount of very beautiful and popular girls headlining it. Jen certainly did not have anyone she really considered a friend. She had practiced and practiced but already felt she'd forgotten her lines. Although it was just a read-through, Ms. Collins encouraged the students to begin memorizing their lines since the play had gotten such a late start. Jen, who was over-achieving by nature, memorized her few lines.

Waiting for her turn, she'd sat on the edge of the stage, legs dangling, staring alternately at her already dog-eared script, and at the dated, patterned green carpet. The closer it came to her turn, the more Jen's stomach twisted in knots. Her left side began to ache. Already feeling ill from womanhood's monthly visit, Jen began feeling downright nauseous at the idea of saying her couple short lines. Vomiting was a real possibility. Jen knew that at least some of her ill feelings were just nerves and she needed to "Man up!" as her Uncle Ed used to say to her cousin Mario.

Alright Jen, you can do this. Let's 'man up,' I mean 'woman up' and do this! Don't get all quiet. Say your lines. You can do it.

It was her turn. What followed was not a result of a lack of trying. Attempting to say the first of her lines with enthusiasm, and enough volume so the director could hear them, made Jen enunciate in this very odd, quick, robotic chirp of her lines "N itfells lick none licks me."

"Can you say that again?" Even Ms. Adam's sounded puzzled.

"Did she say no one *licks me?*" an eleventh grade guy said in disbelief.

This time the same odd, quick, robotic chirp was just louder and more high-pitched. "Nitfells lick none likes me."

Jen's eyes closed shut and remained shut for a moment. She had heard the ridiculously awkward way that her lines came out and was stunned for a moment by how odd it sounded. She wanted to disappear. She repeated it in her mind, over and over hoping that somehow she misheard herself, but each replay only confirmed the inevitable degradation from her peers that would follow. Jen kept her eyes closed and just listened.

"Oh my gosh, what the hell was that!?" said a male voice.

"That's why you don't let a freshman be in a school play," added a girl voice with attitude.

"She sounded like a retarded robot," said another guy with disbelief in his tone.

"No one licks her?! Yeah I bet no one does!" a boy said with a raunchy laugh.

With her eyes still closed, Jen tried to ignore the voices although each one felt like it was ingrained in her mind. The next voice she heard was Ms. Collins.

"Don't worry, honey. You have a few more days to learn your lines. This is only the first rehearsal. You just need to study your lines more and don't be so nervous when you say your lines. Practice enunciating. Just do it like you did in the auditions." Jen knew she was trying to be nice. After what the other students had said, it was hard not to take what Ms. Collins said as anything but condescending.

Jen managed to *enunciate* an "okay" before Ms. Collins moved on to the next scene. Jen got off the stage and quietly told Ms. Collins she was going to the bathroom. In a low voice, the teacher told Jen she could just go home and practice reading her lines if she wanted to. Jen quickly advanced up the graded walk, catching her shoe on the carpet and half tripping near the old wood doorway. Even Mr. Doss who had taken his usual position as door bouncer looked at Jen like he wished he could say something consoling if he knew how to use words. Jen thought she heard a few students laugh but it just as well may have been still echoing in her head. Jen was moving quickly, doing her best not to cry until she got to the bathroom. She turned the corner so quickly that her shoulder clipped the mint green ceramic tile causing her whole body to turn. The pain of a fresh bruise was a small deterrent for someone so close to the release of tears. When she finally walked into the bathroom, she was a dam ready to blow. The cough-choke-cry that poured out was painful, and much louder than Jen expected. Hands on the old white partially cracked porcelain sink, Jen leaned forward letting the facial precipitation drain from her eyes, nose, and mouth into the sink with a low cry for a few seconds before she coughed again and wiped it away, realizing that anyone could walk into the restroom at any time. Jen watched as the drips started to change color, now blackish as the mascara Jen wore made swirled black droplets in the sink.

What is wrong with me? Why couldn't I just say my lines like a normal person? I deserve to have awful things said about me. I wonder if I could just quit the play . . . I'm sure Ms. Collins wouldn't be that heartbroken that her "retarded robot" actress would have to be replaced . . .

Jen was startled by the sound of a bathroom stall door opening. Jen stared at the bottom left side of the mirror horrified to see who was coming out of the stall. Out came a thin, olive-complected girl with short, layered purple hair. She had an empathetic look, but Jen just felt even more embarrassment. Jen looked down again as to not have to make eye contact with the girl. There was little chance the girl didn't hear her from the stall, Jen thought with a roll of her eyes.

Just my luck. Gosh! Why do I always have to cry? I'm stronger than this. Aunt Julie always says you cry because you feel. Why do I always feel so much?

Jen's thoughts were interrupted by the girl now speaking.

"Hi. I'm sorry to bother you but are you okay?" the girl said with consolation in her voice.

"Um, I'm okay. I'm sorry," Jen said, a new wave of tears building, this time out of the frustration that came from embarrassing herself in front of yet another person.

The girl with the purple hair, which Jen could now see had black and pink streaks to it too, just stood there. Then she softly put her hand on Jen's back when the new wave of tears came.

"What happened?" the girl asked supportively.

"Nothing, I, I just, it sounds really stupid but I just did really really bad at play practice, and I was embarrassed. It's fine," Jen said in a voice that became slightly stronger with each word.

"I'm sorry," the girl said reassuringly and empathetically. The girl pursed her lips and moved them to the right as if she was biting her cheek, and looked at Jen like she was searching for the right thing to say to get Jen to stop crying. Jen started to get control of herself.

"I'm okay . . . some of the students can be really mean."

"Yeah most of these kids at this school are a-holes."

"Ha," Jen laughed quietly. "Yeah."

"Hey well I gotta get going," the girl said after looking down at her phone and texting someone back. "You gonna be okay?"

"Yeah."

"If you ever need anything, my name is Sophia."

"Jen."

"See ya, Jen," Sophia said as she left the bathroom.

Jen cleaned herself up and went out to see if her mom was there. Lana was waiting in the car. It was absolutely pouring outside, and Lana reminding Jen that they had church that night with her cheerleader-like enthusiasm did nothing to warm Jen's mood.

Still lying in her bedroom replaying the day, Jen reflected on how nice yet embarrassing and awkward her run-in with Sophia had been before her thoughts were interrupted by Lana's shrill voice.

"Jeeeeennnnnnyyyy. Jeeennnnnyyyy."

"What, Mom?!" Jen said not masking her disdain.

"It's almost time to go. What do you want to eat?"

"I'm not hungry, Mom."

"Jen, you have to eat something."

"I'm not hungry."

"You have to eat something. Do you want a hot peanut butter sandwich?"

"Yes, that's fine," Jen answered to make the conversation stop.

Jen glanced at her watch. It really was almost time to go. A little bit of gratitude creeped into her heart for her mother. Lana must have seen that she needed a few extra minutes to herself. She was usually on Jen's case a lot sooner to leave. As oblivious as she was sometimes, Lana usually was able to grasp if someone was happy, sad, or mad; although it was difficult for her to grasp why someone was anything but happy, as happiness was Lana's default demeanor.

A minute later, Lana was in Jen's room with a hot peanut butter sandwich. Jen noticed how pretty and even normal her mom looked with her tan/ light brown eyeshadow to match her tan/ light brown blouse.

"You look pretty today, Mom."

"Why thank you, Jennifer. We need to get going in a minute."

"Yeah, I will. Thanks, Mom," Jen said looking at her sandwich.

"No problem. Love you, Jenny," Lana said as she exited.

Jen took a bite of the gooey peanut butter noting anew how amazingly better peanut butter sandwiches become when heated. The food was good to Jen and almost immediately made her feel a little stronger, and a half shade less blue.

Chapter 11

The five minute car ride to church passed by slowly in a circular conversation. Lana would say how much she liked Reverend Adam and Jen would say, "Good, Mom." The cycle repeated about a half dozen times until Jen unbuckled her seatbelt, and Lana said, "I'll see you at 8:00." As Jen closed the car door and turned to walk to the old wood and brass paneled door, she heard a faint, "I like Reverend Adam," coming from the car.

Jen rolled her eyes. She looked at her watch and saw she was still ten minutes early. To avoid being the first one to the multipurpose room, Jen walked toward the restroom and took out her iPod touch. She needed to alert social media of her distraughtness. She was ever so happy she'd overheard the church's new Wi-Fi password: "predestination777." Jen had no idea what that meant and wasn't sure how to spell it at first but was ecstatic that her archaic church finally got Wi-Fi. About midway between the front door and the ladies restroom, Jen heard a cheerful voice call her name.

"Jen! It's Jen, right?" Reverend Adam asked, seemingly hopeful that he remembered her name.

"Yeah, it's Jen." Jen again took note of Reverend Adam's clothes. He wore khaki pants and a plain black V-neck T-shirt and the same necklace made of tiny shells Jen had noticed last time.

"Oh okay, Jen. I'm Reverend Adam, but you can just call me Adam. I'm not really used to the "reverend" thing. I know we sorta met the other day but not really . . . "

"Yeah," Jen said, not knowing what to say next.

"Well, it's great to meet you more officially. We're going to get started in just a couple minutes. I guess we're meeting in the multipurpose room. I'll be down there soon."

Jen skipped the trip to the bathroom, and on her way down, messaged Morgan with a one word text, "Help."

The meeting started with chairs all in a circle, which struck Jen as odd. She had never seen that seating arrangement at church. There were only a few chairs in the circle. This was not surprising. One would probably be for her, another for Brian Browning, and whoever else was forced to come. There were about a half dozen chairs. Jen glanced at her iPod to see if Morgan had messaged her back, but she hadn't. Then Jen remembered Morgan was grounded.

Jen's eyes scanned the ugly pattern of beige, brown, and red on the carpet to see a boy standing there. He wore blue jeans that were a little too short, white socks which were more obvious because of the jeans, and white and grey sneakers. He had on an old red T-shirt and thick rimmed glasses. He slouched with his hands in his pockets and his eyes on the floor. The boy looked about Jen's age but seemed even more awkward and out of his element. His hair was brown and disheveled.

He looks jumpy almost like he's physically shaking. He probably has no idea what he's in for. Well maybe he's from a different church, so he does know what he's in for.

A girl with pretty, straight brown hair, skinny jeans and a "Hollister" T-shirt came in walking and laughing with Reverend Adam, who turned to everyone and said, "Good evening, guys! Welcome! Thanks for coming! We're just going to circle up and talk for a few minutes and kind of get to know each other."

During the course of a pretty lame "get to know you" game, Jen learned the jumpy boy's name was Evan and that Madison, the pretty girl from another school, was Reverend Adam's cousin. Brian Browning was as nerdy as ever and considered himself a grandmaster at World of Warcraft, which Jen thought wasn't even a real thing, just something he called himself. Reverend Adam revealed that at one point, he'd wanted to be a professional skateboarder.

Then Reverend Adam began, "Ya know I don't know any of you yet, but I do want to continue to get to know you. Each one of you has a story. A story I would like to hear someday. Ya know, your story can help someone else. That's something that took me a long time to learn. When I was in junior high, I became really angry with life. I was so mad at everything. Most of the time I didn't have a real reason except that I hated being different. I began to hate that I was adopted. I hated my real parents for giving me up for adoption. I hated that I looked different. I hated that I was the only Asian kid in my whole school district. I hated that I always stood out and that everyone always thought I was smart just because I'm Asian, and made squinty eyes at me or called me Chinese or said I was a ninja reject, or literally anything they could think of to insult me. I hated that my adopted parents could never really fully understand me or what I was going through. One day I got so angry when this big dude kept teasing me and punching me in the arm every time he saw me that I shoved him after he hit me in the stairwell. He ended up falling down the stairs and broke his leg. I got kicked out of school. I got in so much trouble. You would think that maybe it felt good to stand up for myself, but even after that, I was still so angry. My parents sent me to a psychiatrist."

Reverend Adam's cousin Madison asked, "Did it help? Going to a psychiatrist?"

"Uhm, well, yeah a little bit but not really. It was actually one day in church when things started to change for me."

Jen rolled her eyes. *Here we go. Yay church. Church is so great. blah blah blah.* However, it wasn't a moment later that Reverend Adam's story piqued Jen's curiosity.

"Yeah, I actually hated going to church and was bored out of my mind . . . " Jen's eyes widened when Reverend Adam confessed he thought church was boring, and she almost let out an audible laugh. God, Himself, only knew how many times Jen was bored out of her mind at church, and hated going. Reverend Shepherd was so, "Church is the best thing in the world all the time yay yay yay," that it was hard to believe someone from the church saying otherwise, even for a moment. Jen glanced at a couple other students, who'd been previously staring at the floor but were now also looking at Reverend Adam with full attention.

" . . . so I was just sitting there in this church service. I hated going and did not want anything to do with it, but my parents had made me go. And I had just run out of paper to draw on so I opened this Bible up that was in the pew. Really just because I was bored out of my mind, not because I actually wanted to read it. Well, I opened it up and it fell to the book of Jeremiah. I remember thinking it was funny because a kid in my class named Jeremiah had recently peed his pants. So anyways, I start reading and it's talking about the nation of Israel or something and all of a sudden I see this verse. I'll never forget it. It said, 'For I know the plans I have for you,' declares the Lord, 'plans to prosper you, not to harm you, plans to give you a hope and a future.' I know that seems like a random verse from the Bible, but I knew for some reason that this verse was talking about me. The actual context of the verse was about the nation of Israel, but I knew that God was also speaking to me at that moment. I don't know how I knew, but I just knew.

I knew that it was God saying that even though my life had hit a pretty rough patch, and even though I was angry and depressed, God still had plans for me. Good things that I would experience later and am still experiencing today. I felt, in that moment, that He hadn't given up on me.

So I'm still in the middle of this church service and ya know, it was crazy. I'm starting to tear up in church of all places. I'm trying to be this tough junior high kid, and the last thing I wanted was someone from my family to see I'm crying and having this moment in church. I wanted my parents to know I hated church, so I did the best I could to keep anyone from noticing, I don't think they noticed but it was something I'll never forget.

Ya know, to be real, it wasn't even that day when things started to change for me. It was a few days later. I kinda put that moment in the back of my mind and was still sorta angry and depressed. But a few days later at my new school, this really quiet kid was getting picked on. He was Black and they called him all kinds of racist names and were just really cruel to him like they were to me at my old school. So I see this kid in the hall, crying by himself after these boys were picking on him. For whatever reason, I think about the verse I had read in church, and I feel bad for the kid. I go over and start talking to him and it turns out he had been adopted too, and he was living with a white family too. Long story short, we became friends.

To this day, Malique is one of my best friends. That was a turning point for my anger to begin to go away. I think there was something about me helping someone else with some of their problems that helped me begin to stop hating myself and others for being different.

There's this other verse in Second Corinthians that says that God comforts us in all our troubles so that we may comfort others with the hope we have in God.

So, sorry to go on and on but that was a story about a time where I was able to help someone else because of something that happened to me. Sometimes we think 'I'm not special, there's not anything I can do.' But the reality is that God made you how you are; He made you special. Whether you believe that or think that's lame or whatever. It doesn't make it any less true. I feel like I've been babbling on forever, so I'll end with this. I hope that is something you are able to realize, that you are special and God does have great plans for your life. You never know the people you might be able to help."

Reverend Adam closed in prayer. Although the prayer was shorter than many she had experienced at church, Jen really wasn't listening. She was puzzled at Reverend Adam's story. He seemed so normal. So not church-like, yet his story was clearly very religious. It also struck Jen that Reverend Adam thought God spoke to him. *Just an odd thought, God the silent one up in the sky, communicating to someone. I mean Reverend Adam seems cool and all, but was he a little crazy? Reverend Adam didn't seem crazy, so if God really talked to him. Why him? Why was God silent toward me? Toward my mom? Reverend Adam probably just had a breakdown or something or maybe he just thought his own weird thoughts were God. Just like our church, to bring in someone crazy to work with teens.*

Chapter 12

S ometimes melancholy has a smell. To Jen, it smelled like cheap men's aftershave. An old country farmer at the grocery store wearing a red flannel brought the fragrance of memories and quickly became victim to Jen's disapproving glare. The man appeared puzzled, snapping Jen back to the present. The man she really wanted to glare at was John Morris. Johnny, as he was known to those who were close to him, was Jen's father. Jen had only interacted with her father for three brief periods in her life.

The first period, which Jen remembered the least, stretched across the first six months of her life. Jen remembered this period of her life secondhand, through stories she'd heard from her Aunt Julie and Lana and from piecing different photographs together.

According to Lana, Johnny loved Jen so much he felt he'd best help his family by moving out West to make money. They didn't have much back then. Jen once overheard Aunt Julie tell their neighbor that Johnny was a womanizer. Despite being married to Lana for just over a year, he couldn't handle her. He convinced Lana he was leaving "for the good of the family," and that he would "send money as soon as he made his fortune." Aunt Julie made the last two statements with air quotes, rolled eyes, and shakes of her head, unaware Jen was listening, peeking through the crack of a slightly open door.

The only other memento from this time was a photo of Johnny holding her as an infant. Sitting on an old beige couch with yellow and brown plaid couch cushions, he had slicked back hair, a white tank top style undershirt and blue jeans with holes in them. Johnny gave a half smile to the photographer. It made her wonder if there was a part of her dad that did like being a dad. Was there a part of him that did like her? Or was the smile a mirage, like the idea of having a father in one's life.

The second period of Johnny in Jen's life was when she was about four. Despite Jen being so young, Jen remembered the happiness. She remembered the laughs of her young mom, the smiles coming from two sets of mouths, not just one. She remembered her dad tossing her up in the air and catching her with strong arms. Aunt Julie even got a picture of Jen falling mid-air from a toss still two inches from her dad's arms, hair still flowing in the wind. The smile on Jen's face was so wide that her little face barely contained it. Their family was complete. Johnny had even brought money when he returned. He brought $700 with him. It was not really that much money back then, and it certainly wasn't that much money considering it took Johnny three years to earn it. It was, however, a lot of money to Lana who was very proud of Johnny.

Besides the happiness, the other thing Jen remembered vividly were her tears. Jen was sent to her Aunt Julie's house, who still lived in Ohio at the time, so her mom and dad could talk. At Aunt Julie's house, she told Jen her dad was leaving and probably wasn't coming back, Jen cried for hours and hours until she couldn't cry anymore and had pains in her chest. It was the first time it had ever happened and Jen never forgot it. When she got back from Aunt Julie's house, she found her home emptier. Lana admitted to Jen that her daddy had left, something that Aunt Julie had already shared with her. Lana spent the next half an hour reassuring and crying with Jen, but there was something about her mom's tears that she knew he wasn't coming back. When Jen finally stopped crying again she heard Lana say, "Jen, don't worry Daddy's going down South only for a couple weeks just to make some money, then he'll be back with us."

He returned a couple weeks after Jen's tenth birthday, 316 weeks later to be exact. Not that Jen ever counted or anything, except the day she was bored in sixth grade math, and she did count.

There were a few things that were much different about seeing her father for the third time. First, Jen remembered everything. Jen remembered when she yelled up to her mom that there was a strange man at the door holding flowers, a Barbie doll, and a baseball glove. She remembered the aftershave. She remembered the way she, even at ten years old, thought her dad looked fake when he made promises, the same ones that her mom still seemed to believe freely.

The strangest dynamic this time around was Ronnie. He'd been conceived the last time Johnny had been home when Jen was four, and since Johnny had not been back since, this was Ronnie's first and only interaction with his dad. An odd and complex set of emotions ran through her. She loved seeing Ronnie so happy. She loved watching her often bored six-year-old brother play catch with a dad. She also hated watching her often bored six-year-old brother play catch with a dad that could leave at any moment. During Johnny's stay, Jen felt a strange combination of relief-joy and/or of anger-resentment. These emotions changed with such an incredible frequency, they made her feel like a wreck inside.

She recalled one thirty second time period where she'd cried tears of joy, followed by tears of anger. It was a couple days after Johnny's return. Jen had been distant with her father ever since he'd returned. After a day or so, Lana began to notice that Jen had been abnormally quiet. As she left for school, Lana advised Jen to open up her heart to her dad. Jen thought about her mom's advice all day at school, finally deciding she didn't need a dad and was going to tell him that when she got home. Sure enough, Jen got off her bus and saw Johnny sitting on the porch. Jen marched off the bus determined to give Johnny a piece of her mind. She stepped off the bus and moved stride by stride toward Johnny, but Johnny beat her to it.

"Jenny, I swear there could not be a prettier girl in this whole county. With your long brown hair and big brown eyes, I'm going to have to get a shotgun to fight off all the boys that'll be coming your way."

This caught Jen off-guard, and it made her really look at Johnny for the first time. He smiled widely and looked directly at Jen. He was still wearing his patent white T-shirt but at least it looked new and his jeans didn't have rips in them like Jen had seen in the pictures. His slicked back hair now had small streaks of grey and that made him look a bit more mature but no less handsome. She let him hug her. Feeling his embrace made Jen remember how happy she was as a kid. That twitch of strong emotion made Jen's eyes well up and she was glad that Johnny's smiling gaze was interrupted by Ronnie running up and jumping in Johnny's arms. It was this jumping into Johnny's strong arms that was the second time Jen was overcome with emotions. This time the vivid memory and pictures of Johnny throwing Jen up in the air combined with her seeing Ronnie thrown in the air only to be caught by Johnny's strong arms made Jen angry. Angry that her father left and let her crash down to the fatherless, insecure earth.

Jen began to open up and talk some more with her father and even initiated a hug with him for the first time in years that brought tears of relief but the relief only lasted about thirty-six hours until Johnny let everyone know that he would be moving on to get more work. This time "a buddy" of his said Texas was where all the work was these days. This time Jen did not cry but was so angry she did not eat for two days. It wasn't until Morgan invited her to a theme park a day later Jen finally got back to normal. Sometimes Jen wondered what revelries awaited Johnny in Texas that were so incredible as to abandon his own flesh and blood. The more Jen thought about it, she realized that "Texas vs Family" is only a difficult decision if you value your family, and Jen knew that wasn't the case with her father.

Lana took things differently this time. Despite years of optimism toward the idea of Johnny returning, she was much less optimistic this time. While Lana still would not admit to the probable fact that Johnny wasn't coming back at least for another half dozen years or so, she did have a more sobered countenance when talking about Johnny. She looked sadder, and while Lana did not have the strongest ability to read people, she did notice her children, especially Ronnie.

Ronnie almost failed first grade. He asked every single day when his dad was coming back. Six months straight. He couldn't do school work. His teacher said he cried every day in class. He said he felt sick every morning. Lana, Mrs. Algeo, and Principal Mongenel had to have an end-of year-conference to determine whether Ronnie would pass first grade.

What Aunt Julie said later stuck with Jen. "Everyone always thinks that what they do doesn't matter. That all the decisions they make only affect themselves. But *every* decision affects others. Decisions have casualties."

Sometimes Jen felt like a casualty.

Chapter 13

It was third period World History, which used to be Jen's favorite class because she shared it with Morgan. However, Morgan had been absent four days in a row, which was odd because Jen could've sworn she'd seen Morgan in the hallway that morning, walking with Zoey Davidson. The bell rang and now she was stuck in Mr. Harris's class, Morganless.

Mr. Harris began class: "You need to complete this map of the countries of Africa, complete with capitals. Make sure that you properly label each country and capital. There will not be room for you to write the name of every country in its location on the map. Just make sure you label clearly with an arrow or a line to show where they are located. If I can't read it, you're not getting credit for it. You can work with a partner. Just make sure it gets done."

Jen quickly glanced around the room in case Morgan had come in late. Her thoughts were interrupted when a voice from two seats over shouted with equal parts volume and annoyance, "Hi Jonifer!"

"Jordan what do you *want?*"

"Where's your best friend from Camp Rock?"

"I don't know. She's probably out plotting your doom."

"Ha ha I'm not scared."

"You should be."

"*You* should be."

"Wow, you can be quiet now."

"Wow, *you* can be quiet now!"

Jen raised her hand. "Mr. Harris, what's this country here on the far side of Africa."

"That's Mozambique," Mr. Harris said in an even, educational tone.

"Yeah, can we send Jordan here to Mozambique?" Jen asked in a pleading voice.

"Ya know, I already looked into it. I had that same idea a few weeks ago and turns out they don't want him either. Turns out they have a ban against annoying students who don't do their work. Sorry. Disappointing, isn't it?" Mr. Harris said, beginning with a straight face that faded into a big smile.

Jen laughed and laughed, a little surprised that Mr. Harris had said something that was actually funny. Who knew that was possible? Jen moved to an empty seat and spent the rest of class studying her map of Africa, smiling when she spotted Mozambique. Meanwhile, Jordan and Mr. Harris argued back and forth for twenty minutes. Their discussion points could be best summarized as, "Teachers aren't allowed to talk about students like that," versus "Students aren't allowed to be irritating and not do their work."

When the bell rang, Jen sprang to the door hungry and hoping to have enough time to finish her lunch today. The hallway was a set of dueling rivers: one river flowing toward the cafeteria, the other churning away from it. Students floated like leaves caught in the current. They sometimes switched tributaries once their friends/boyfriends/girlfriends streamed into their classrooms. Sections of the river moved fast or slow depending on who you walked behind. Jen definitely preferred the fast section, since she did not consider the hallway a place to be social. Jen wanted to get from point A to point B as quickly as possible. She floated past the pooled up places behind dams of students: a couple embracing, kissing and seemingly grinding so hard on each other that they looked as if they were attempting to start a family in the hallway; other groups of students vending cell phones, video games, Yu-gi-oh cards, and what Jen thought looked like prescription meds.

Just as she thought she might actually get to lunch before the lines were annoyingly long, the girls she had been following stopped abruptly, causing Jen to almost run into them. Jen spun, looking to go around them and ran right into Chance, the red-headed kid from her bus.

"Geez, now you're walking like a retard!" Chance said with a laugh.

"Shut up!"

"Ha ha!" Chance laughed in Jen's face.

Jen shoved him and walked away.

What the heck is wrong with people!? Why do people have to say stuff? There's nothing I can do about my mom. I can't win. Luckily, it's just this idiot. I'm sure that Chance's family isn't exactly ivy league material, but still. Jen refused to think about it anymore.

As she continued down the graded hallway to the gym, an interesting pattern on the opposite side of the wall-to-wall people caught her eye. It was a circle of dark-light, dark-light, dark-light, with light brown in the middle. Jen realized peoples' heads formed the pattern. It made slightly more sense when she saw that it was Drake walking in the middle of six girls. Two girls walked ahead of him, glancing back and laughing every few steps. He had a girl on either side of himside and two walking behind in perfect symmetry. Drake turned to talk to the girls behind him every few seconds. There were three blondes and three with silky-black dark hair. Two of the girls had curly hair and four of them straight. All were beautiful and made up perfectly. Jen doubted that Drake had purposely arranged them like that but it was still ridiculous that the girls apparently were oblivious to the fact that they were walking in such a perfect light and shadow symmetrical contrast. As they were heading the opposite way, Jen caught a glimpse of the last blonde and dark-haired girls bringing up the rear of Drake's harem. It was Morgan and Zoey Davidson. Part of Jen wanted to say hello, but they seemed so far away in the crowd of students, so she just kept walking. *I'm sure the last thing Morgan would want is her uncool friend embarrassing her in front of Drake. I know she probably doesn't want to be bothered. I feel like if we were back in eighth grade she'd still want me to stop and say hi to her. Crazy to think that was just six months ago. A lot can change in six months . . .*

After school, play practice went much better. Jen had gotten used to saying her lines to the point that only occasionally kids would mock her about her first practice line reading. Jen left school in a good mood, even despite the knowledge she had another young people's meeting that night.

Reverend Adam referred to these meetings as "youth group." Youth group had been going pretty well the last few weeks. While Jen probably wouldn't go if she wasn't being coerced, all in all the meetings were really pretty painless. That was a vast improvement from anything she had ever experienced at church as a whole. It was still located at their boring church. They still played games or did activities that were kinda lame but they were slightly better than any Jen had done in school. However, there were a couple things that were much better than before.

First, there were more students than ever before. It wasn't a lot of students, it wasn't even enough to fit a school classroom, but there were like fifteen to twenty or so students that had begun coming to these meetings every week. Some of the same annoying students came like Brian Browning and a couple of his friends, but there were others too. Reverend Adam's cousin Madison continued to come from McEntyre High and started to bring a couple of her friends, also very pretty and stylish. While Jen didn't really click with them, they were pleasant enough. An eleventh grader named Kaitlyn and her boyfriend Ben came. They mostly just talked or argued with each other. While Jen didn't talk to them much, she enjoyed listening to their banter. Evan, the jumpy kid Jen had met at the first meeting, kept coming and he started to bring his best friend Justin. Evan seemed much less nervous with Justin there, and it was obvious that he was just pretty shy.

Most interestingly, there were six to eight students Reverend Adam had met at the park, which Jen couldn't decide if that was weird or cool. Jen pieced together that he'd spotted these kids skateboarding at the park. He'd struck up a conversation and then took them out for lunch or brought them lunch, and then he'd invited them and they actually came. They definitely did not seem to have ever been to church before. They cussed and talked about all the bad things they did. Lana would have flipped. They skateboarded in the church parking lot, wrestled each other for fun, and unlike Jen had absolutely no fear of saying something inappropriate in front of Reverend Shepherd. On several occasions a perturbed Reverend Shepherd called Reverend Adam to come talk to him in his office after youth group. They seemed so far from the normal church people. Jen thought it was interesting that most of the new members of youth group had families that did not even attend First Congregational Community Church.

Probably the most tolerable thing about youth group was Adam himself and his wife Lindsey. They just seemed so young and cool and nice. They were just so "chill" as Morgan would say. They did not seem annoyed or angry when they heard the skater kids cuss or talk about inappropriate things. They just nicely reminded them that they were in church, and to keep things church appropriate. While Reverend Shepherd looked shocked and disappointed, Adam and Lindsey took it in stride and didn't seem to think any less of the students that were a little rough around the edges. They just seemed to genuinely care about them. They knew movies and music, had iPhones, and were not even slightly traditional in the way they looked or dressed. Adam and Lindsey seemed to sincerely love and annoy each other in the way she had only ever seen from her Aunt Julie and her Uncle Ed. Jen was continually surprised by how fun and kind Adam and Lindsey were. They seemed so real. There was something about them that Jen wanted more of. It was hard for Jen to put her finger on what it was that she liked about them, but the more she thought about it, it was that she felt like they really cared about her and everyone. Jen had other people who cared about her, but there was something about how they cared without pitying that appealed to Jen. Jen remembered one specific conversation she'd had with Lindsey:

"Jen, I love your shirt. It looks so soft and comfy."

"Oh, thanks."

"So how's school and play practice and everything? Is it going any better?

"Yeah, it is. It's good enough that I'm not noticed anymore, which is good."

"Ha, that's funny. Yeah sometimes under the radar is good. Stuff going okay at home?"

"Yeah . . . " Jen answered with a little hesitation in her voice.

"Reverend Shepherd told us a little about your family. I'm sure it can be tough, but ya know I think God knew what He was doing. I think He put the right young woman who is strong enough to be in your position. You seem like you're doing a great job with everything, although I'm sure it's tough."

"Yeah I guess . . . " Jen responded unconvincingly.

Adam, who was close enough, that at one point Jen wondered if he was eavesdropping, ended his conversation with another student and said to Jen, "That's right! You're strong! You got this, girl!" He flexed his muscles in demonstration.

"And seriously though, if you ever need anything, Adam and I are always here for you. Even if you just need to go get coffee and take a break. Wait, do you drink coffee?"

"Ah . . . no," Jen answered with a smile.

"Tea?" Lindsey asked with a hopeful smile.

"Yeah, tea," Jen said smiling back.

"Okay, tea or lunch or whatever."

"Yeah, and when is your play again?" Adam interjected.

"November thirteenth, fourteenth, and fifteenth."

"Excellent! We'll be there with bells on!" Adam said with an awkward expression on his face.

"Bells on? Really, Adam?" Lindsey asked.

"Yeah. That's what closers say Linds," Adam said laughing.

"Okay, Gus . . . Wellll . . . that's my husband," Lindsey said with a deep audible sigh, eye roll, head shake, and smile.

Lying awake in bed, Jen kept coming back to what Lindsey had said to her about God knowing what he was doing and that she was strong enough to be in her position. It was odd for Jen to think of herself as strong enough. Almost every day Jen felt like she wasn't up for the challenge. She felt like she couldn't do it. Every time she felt like life was finally going okay, Lana or someone else or even Jen herself would do something to make her lose whatever feeling of life competency she had. Yet, of all the people she knew, she wasn't sure anyone else could do what she did, even though she didn't know if she could do what she did. She pondered the possibility that she actually was the right person to handle the struggles of her life.

Chapter 14

Friday brought some much-needed sunshine. It had been a rainy beginning to the fall. While it wasn't a cold, bone-chilling rain like they sometimes got in Western Ohio, it was nonetheless wet, and Jen was sick of it. The sunshine matched Jen's countenance. She was feeling upbeat this Friday. Jen still had not been able to get a hold of Morgan. Last she had heard, Morgan was grounded and that was about three and a half weeks ago. Since Jen had met Morgan in second grade, the longest she'd ever been grounded was a couple days. Jen wondered whether Morgan was still grounded or if she was just ghosting her. However, this Friday Jen had plans to hang out with her friend Britta from Jefferson High School.

Jen and Britta played tennis together last summer when they worked at Jefferson Country Club. It had been a couple months since they had hung out so Jen was happy to catch up and to actually spend time with someone that wasn't Lana or Ronnie, especially since Morgan had been MIA. While Jen and Britta didn't really hang out very much since they went to different schools, Jen liked that they always picked up right where they left off. Jen hopped off the bus and went inside. As she was putting her backpack down, she heard the phone ring. Thinking it was probably Lana, she reluctantly grabbed it.

"Hello."

"Hello, Jen?"

"Hey, Britta! How's it going?"

"Ummm . . . not good. Apparently, my lame parents have relatives coming in from out of town. They completely did not tell me either! Or maybe they did, but I wasn't listening. They're always rambling on about stupid stuff. Jen, I'm so sorry. My parents are ridiculous."

Jen's heart sank. She didn't say anything. She didn't know what to say.

"Jen, are you still there?"

"Yeah, sorry, yeah that sucks. I'm sorry."

"Yeah, well, we'll hang out soon. I'll message you next week and we'll hang out soon."

"Yeah," Jen said unenthusiastically.

"Alright, well, I gotta jet. My parents are making me clean. Bye."

"Bye."

Jen ran upstairs and fell onto her bed. She lay there facedown, angry and disappointed.

The one time I have plans to actually enjoy my life, my friend cancels. That about sums up my life.

Jen lay on her bed, drinking in her sadness. Eventually, she could feel herself falling asleep.

Not twenty minutes later, Jen awoke to Lana calling her. She didn't even know that her mom was home. She felt startled and annoyed that her mom needed her.

Can't I just be sad and alone? I have to be annoyed too?

Lana kept calling. Jen finally answered, wondering why her mom couldn't just come up the stairs.

"What, Mom?" Jen yelled with extra anger in her voice.

"Jenny! The phone is for you! Phone!"

Ugh . . . I don't feel like talking to anybody. Well it could be Britta uncanceling. Jen's hopes rose at the thought of possibly still being able to hang out with Britta, so she dashed downstairs.

Lana met her with the phone.

"It's Lindsey, Reverend Adam's wife!" Lana said with big eyes and a cheesy smile to match.

Jen shook her head as Lana handed her the phone. At that moment, she wished Lana was like Morgan's mom who had no problem telling people Morgan wasn't home when Morgan was standing right there but didn't want to talk. Jen knew that nothing she could say would prevent Lana from handing her the phone. She grabbed the phone in defeat.

"Hello," Jen said, trying not to sound annoyed.

"Hey, Jen. I hope this isn't a bad time. This is Lindsey, Reverend Adam's wife from church."

"Oh hey," Jen said nonchalantly.

"So I was wondering if you weren't busy, maybe we could go grab tea or if you're feeling really adventurous, we can grab dinner. I'm kinda hungry. Are you hungry?"

"Ah, yeah, I guess," Jen said agreeably.

"Okay, are you hungry for anything in particular? Do you have a favorite restaurant in the area?"

"No not really."

"How about Mexican?"

"Yeah, that sounds fine."

"Okay, cool. Can I talk to your mom real quick?"

Jen passed the phone to her mom and listened.

"Ohhhh, Yeah! Jenny would love to go to eat with you . . . Yeah she's so special. Oh, yeah you can pick her up whenever you want. No, *thank you*! Okay bye, thank you. Thanks. Bye. Bye."

Jen couldn't help but shake her head as her mom spoke on the phone. Her embarrassment soon gave way to nervousness of going and meeting Lindsey. Lindsey seemed nice enough, but Jen felt like she still didn't really know her.

I mean she's from church, so she has that going against her. She does seem cool when I talk to her at church for a couple minutes, but this is like a whole meal just her and me and what if she talks to me and is weird and she starts lecturing me for liking Star Wars again or something . . . or if I somehow breathe unChristian-like or whatever . . . I just don't know . . .

Jen was about to tell her mom that she wasn't feeling well, and that she would have to cancel with Lindsey when her mom announced that Lindsey would be there in two minutes.

"Two minutes? Already? I thought we were meeting later!"

"No she said she would be here around 4:30."

Jen glanced over at the clock: 4:28.

"Mom! Why didn't you tell me three minutes ago that she was coming now?"

"Oh, I thought she told you."

"No, she just said today!"

"Oh, sorry. I'm happy she's coming. I think it is so good for you to have another friend, like an adult friend in your life."

Jen barely heard the last part of what Lana said as she ran upstairs to change. She had no idea what to wear. She didn't really want to wear what she wore to school, but she didn't know. Instead she went into the bathroom to fix her hair and redo the little bit of makeup she wore. She didn't know why she cared yet her mom had trained her that social interactions with others were important. All in all, Jen did consider Lindsey and Adam to be relatively cool compared with most church people.

Lindsey's Honda pulled in about five minutes later. Jen became more nervous when she stepped into Lindsey's car.

"Hey, Jen! How are you?"

"Oh, I'm fine, I guess."

"Yeah? That's good," Lindsey said reassuringly. "So is this restaurant 'Tulum' good?"

"I don't know, I've never been there. I've heard it's good, though. We don't really go out to eat much."

"That's okay. Home-cooked meals are always better anyways."

"Yeah."

Their car pulled into the new or recently renovated Tulum restaurant. Jen thought the decor was kind of interesting. It had faux stonework like it was archaeological ruins or something. Jen also noted the floor was not completely unlike an archaeological dig, but instead of dirt and dust, there were bits of food and tortilla chips. Jen was happy to see it was centered around only one table that looked like it held debris from small children. A young woman headed to the 'dig site' with a sweeper. They walked to a much cleaner table by a window. As they sat down, Jen glanced out the window at the red maple that was about halfway through donating its leaves in honor of autumn.

Lindsey peered over her menu and smiled at Jen and asked, "So how are things? I know I just saw you like two days ago at youth group but ya know, I didn't get to really talk to you. Are you excited about the play?"

"Uhm . . . yeah . . . " Jen said unconvincingly.

"I think I would be so nervous."

"Yeah," Jen said, shaking her head in agreement.

"I never really did any theater productions but I did sing in choir and did band."

"Really?"

"Yeah, ha, high school is so crazy sometimes. I remember being so competitive with choir and band."

"Really?"

"Yeah I remember one time there was this girl Cindy Carson. She used to get all the solos at the choir concerts. She was so pretty and she did have a good voice, but it was like any solo automatically went to her. They barely had tryouts. They just like gave it to her. Ha, I got so mad I went and like yelled at the choir teacher after class, and told her I was going to report her. I don't know to whom but . . . ha ha yeah it was so crazy."

"Really?" Jen doubted the idea that Cindy got the part because she was pretty as she thought that Lindsey was very pretty herself, but she smiled as Lindsey continued.

They ordered and moments later the waiter brought chips and salsa.

"Thank you," Lindsey said to the waiter looking right at him.

"Thanks," Jen said smiling, remembering that she should probably thank him as well.

Lindsey spooned the salsa on to her chip, and took a bite.

"Mmmmm . . . salsa is delicious."

"Yeah," Jen said surprised at how good the salsa tasted despite her mouth feeling like it was partly burning.

"The craziest part of all this is that when I finally got the solo at the concert, my voice cracked right at the most important part and completely messed it up. It was so embarrassing. The funny thing about high school is it was a huge deal at the time but all in all, it's not really a big deal. High school was kinda lame."

"Yeah, ha, it is." Jen didn't know if it was just the spicy but delicious salsa or her story of her insecure high school self, but she felt like she started to like Lindsey even more. She seemed less of a weird church person, and more like a real person, like someone you would want as a friend.

Jen thoroughly enjoyed the tacos they ordered as she had not had tacos from a restaurant not named Taco Bell in a while.

"So Jen, tell me more about yourself. What do you enjoy doing besides eating tacos and advancing your career on Broadway . . . ," Lindsey said with a smile.

"Ha, yeah I'm not sure about the Broadway thing, but I don't know, I like to watch TV, read and such."

"Yeah, read, huh? That seems to be a lost art. I feel like most students your age just watch Netflix and play video games, not many read anything besides their homework and social media feeds. What do you like to read?"

"It's kinda old, and my mom always thinks it's weird that I like her so much, but I love Agatha Christie."

"Yeah, girl!" Lindsey said with enthusiasm as she held out her hand to give Jen five. "That is amazing. I absolutely love Agatha Christie. She has the most incredible twists and turns, and I feel like her characters are all very likeable, ya know until she inevitably kills them off."

"Yeah, like I read enough of her books, that I should know who the killer is. Yet so often I'm totally wrong and it's someone random that I didn't expect."

"So what's your favorite one?"

"*Murder on the Orient Express.*"

"Yeah, it's so good, like what story has an ending like that?! Crazy. I just read one of her books, and I won't tell you which one so I don't give it away, but the whole story is told as the confession of the murderer. But you don't know that until like the very end of the book. It's so crazy."

"Yeah, she's awesome like that. My mom always thinks it's weird that I always want to read about people getting murdered, but I think it's interesting."

"Yeah like I always tell Adam, I can think of so many ways to kill him now," Lindsey laughed

"Yeah like poison salsa!" Jen said with a gleam in her eye before they both busted up laughing.

"Wow, I was not expecting that, Jen. Uhmmm . . . waiter, check please!" Lindsey said to the waiter that wasn't there.

Jen just laughed and laughed.

"So you're welcome to go ahead and eat the rest of the salsa and . . . Actually . . . on second thought, maybe we can box that up. I'll take it home for my husband. That's the least I can do, really," Lindsey said with a laugh.

Jen and Lindsey left the restaurant giggling. Lindsey gave Jen a big hug and wished Jen luck and told her she was excited to see her play. Jen left Lindsey's car happy to have had a much nicer time than she'd ever imagined.

Chapter 15

J en had anxiety toward most things in life. She was anxious before class; she was anxious during class and after. She was anxious in social situations; she was anxious thinking about the *possibility* of being in social situations. The anxiety she had the night before the play was almost crippling. The three-hour, day-before-opening-night play practice unfortunately did not end Jen's anxiousness. The only slight distraction was the big package she found on their doorstep when she got home.

Jennifer Morris
203 Vine Street
Hemlock Ridge, Ohio
45340

Julie Cerrone
28305 Gainsley Dr.
Sterling Heights, Michigan
48313

Lana came over as Jen carried the package inside. Jen's eyes grew wide and a slight smile lit her face when she saw the package was from Sterling Heights, Michigan.

"What is it, Jenny?" Lana asked inquisitively.

"It's a package from Aunt Julie!" she said with a smile.

Jen found the side folds in the brown paper packaging. She ripped it off and found a note and a shoebox with the words "Sophique" written in script.

"Sorry, I won't be able to make it this weekend! :-(I hope these come in handy for your big debut! XOXO, Aunt Julie."

Jen opened the shoebox to find a pair of gorgeous shiny black heels. They had a medium high heel, enough to look very grown up and chic but not so high that it looked like she was trying too hard. The tip of the toe was more pointed than the average heel and instead of a full back to the heel there was a sling-back ankle strap with a small gold buckle. They were absolutely perfect. A big grin spread across Jen's face as she stared in awe of the shoes. Part of Jen was excited to wear them, and part of Jen felt overwhelmed, wondering whether she could pull them off.

"Wow, Jenny, those are beautiful!" Lana said in awe.

"Yeah . . . " Jen said breathlessly. Jen wasn't even really a shoe girl, but there was something about this pair of heels that made Jen feel sophisticated. She imagined herself wearing them to a red carpet event at a New York museum or some other fancy event. "You better send Aunt Julie a thank you note."

"Yeah, I should."

Jen brought her backpack and the shoes up to her room and put the box on top of her dresser in a place of honor before heading back downstairs to do her homework. She put her school items on the kitchen table, sat down, and began her biology homework for next week. "What are you working on, Jenny?" Lana asked.

"Just some biology homework."

"You going to be able to get it done?"

"Yeah it's for next week and it's not that hard."

"That's good," Lana said as she began to get out pots and pans and opened a large new book that she put on the counter.

"Are you nervous about the play tomorrow?"

"Yeah," Jen didn't particularly want to divulge this information to her mother, but there was no possible stretch of the truth that made the answer anything but, yes she was nervous.

Lana didn't respond but got the skillet out and began to sear some kind of meat, and cut up some apples. Lana usually had a response to everything, so this struck Jen as strange, but it wasn't enough to prompt Jen to talk more about it.

"Dinner is going to be delicious, Jenny."

"Yeah?" Jen said, not as sure.

"Yep. I'm trying out a new cookbook."

"Okay, sounds good. Make sure you follow all the directions."

"Ya know, Jenny, I've been cooking long before you were born," Lana said with confidence.

"Ha ha okay, Mom. I'm excited to try it."

"Jenny, why don't we relax and watch a movie tonight?"

"Yeah?" Jen said, not opposed to taking her mind off the play the next day.

"Yeah, why don't we watch one of the classics. I brought home *An Affair to Remember*. We haven't seen it in a while . . . "

"Yeah, ok."

"After all, Jenny, 'Winter is cold for those that have no warm memories,'" Lana said in her best Deborah Kerr impression.

"Ha, that's true."

"Mom, Mom! Woo woo! What we eatin' fo'dinner?" Ronnie said, running into the kitchen shouting.

"I'm not sure you get dinner if you shout at your mother."

"Oh, come on! Watch me whip, whip, watch me nae-nae! Watch me, watch me!" Ronnie exhorted unmusically, accompanying his exclamation with uncoordinated movements.

"Really, Ronnie? That song is so old!" Jen said.

"Yeah? Watch me whip, whip, watch me nae-nae!" Ronnie sang.

"Ronnie, I'm not sure you could sound more Caucasian," Jen said.

"I don't care Jen-nay! Woo-woo!" Ronnie skipped out of the room as he bubbled with energy.

"Geez, how much sugar did he have today?" Jen asked, shaking her head.

"He's not much of a Cary Grant type, is he?" Lana responded, also shaking her head.

"No, he's not," Jen said with a giggle, met with Lana's own giggles.

Lana nailed dinner. She followed the recipe to a tee and it turned out delicious. The pork chops were juicy and flavorful.

The apple seemed to really complement the pork. Jen decided she should start learning how to cook.

Jen spent the evening cuddling with her mom on the couch. The movie was one of Jen and Lana's favorites. Ronnie decided to play his handheld video game in his room, instead of watching.

As the credits rolled, Lana quoted the movie: "Jenny if you can paint, I can walk! Anything can happen don't you think?"

"Mom, I can't paint and you can already walk."

"It's a miracle!"

Jen laughed as her mom hugged her and held her tight for a minute.

"Jenny, I'm so proud of you! You're going to do so great tomorrow!"

Jen smiled and let her mom hold her an extra few seconds.

After school Friday, the cast of the play did a quick run-through, followed by a ninety minute break before they had to be back at school to get ready.

Jen returned to mayhem at school. Students were running around trying to find their places and costumes. Others were on their phones livestreaming that they were "freaking out" because some important members of the play hadn't arrived yet. All seemed like chaos, even Mr. Doss looked flustered trying to keep craziness in check. Jen went to look for an extra script just to review her lines again for the 10,000th time before the play started. As she reached for what she thought were the extra scripts Jen almost bumped into Ms. Collins, "Oh, hey, Jen! You all ready?" Ms. Collins looked Jen up and down with a quizzical expression. "Oh, those are the shoes that you are going to wear? Remember, you're supposed to have low self-esteem. They look rather self-assured. Well just try to walk in them awkwardly. You know, like you're not very confident wearing heels."

"Oh . . . ah . . . okay," Jen replied with a nervous chuckle unsure on what exactly that would entail. "Oh, and Ms. Collins, where are the extra scripts?"

"Oh just over on that table over there." Ms. Collins pointed to a rectangular fold-up table on the opposite side of the room.

"Okay, thanks," Jen said, as she started walking toward the other table.

"Oh, and Jen great job. You're walking in those perfectly! Just like that on stage! Nice and awkward!" Ms. Collins called to Jen.

Jen scrunched her face and added a half-hearted, "Ok, thanks . . . " as she had not begun trying to walk awkwardly. *I guess it's good I'm just naturally awkward . . .*

Chapter 16

Showtime finally arrived. The lights were down. The orchestra played. The curtain opened. Jen was in the first act and was happy that she could get to finish her lines at the beginning and not have to nervously wait all play. After that, she really only had a few parts where she was on stage in the background, and once, walking depressed-like with two other students across the stage. *Easy enough.*

They were about thirty minutes into the play. Somehow, the minutes ticked by both quickly and slowly. With each scene, a new wave of anxiety came over Jen. *It's closer. It's almost time.*

Jen felt like she could hardly breathe during the scene before hers. Jen was waiting with the two other students in the same scene as hers when Ms. Collins walked up to her.

"Jen, are you ready?" she said in a calm and hushed voice, which still somehow startled Jen, even though she saw her walk over.

"Ah, yeah."

"Just like we practiced! Be the part! You can do it!"

"Okay."

Jen found it comforting that she entered the stage with two other students, upperclassmen. Although they both exited after their lines, leaving her alone on stage, at least she didn't have to walk on stage alone. Jen noted how bright the lights were as the three of them walked on stage. Luckily she didn't have to go first. Jen stood stage left next to a prop wall just as they had practiced. She stood waiting for the upperclassman named Kyle to begin his lines. Jen began to give a nervous smile until she remembered to be in character and quickly frowned.

"Ya know, it's not my fault I'm so cool, popular, and good at sports. I don't face much rejection but when I do it's for being *too* cool, popular, and good at sports. People are like 'oh you're life is so easy.' Like it's something I should feel bad about. Well, ya know what? I don't feel bad. I'm not going to apologize for being good at life!" Kyle said with convincing arrogance.

Next a sophomore named Paige playing the part of "Sarah the Socialite" read her line: "'You shouldn't have so many boyfriends, Sarah. You don't have to jump from boyfriend to boyfriend, Sarah.' I can't help that I'm a hot commodity! I like being liked. Why should I suppress who I am?"

It was her turn.

She started: "They tell me everyone is important but sometimes I just don't feel like it. I feel like nothing. Sometimes, I just sit alone in my room and cry."

Jen said her lines convincingly, with good annunciation and volume. Jen turned to leave, happily relieved that she did her part without problem.

Then it happened. Whether it was from an old chair, a piece of the stage, lighting, props or simply dropped from the sky, there it was, a simple metal screw. As Jen turned to exit, she placed the forefoot of one of her new heels directly onto the screw. The screw, as if made of ice, slipped out from under Jen's right foot. Jen's right leg followed and slid out from under her, as her body flung awkwardly to the ground. Her right hand caught something sharp from the corner of a fake wall as she tried to keep herself from falling, and her head hit the ground. She wasn't really hurt. Yes, her head, knee, rear, and hand ached but it was obvious to Jen that she wasn't seriously hurt. She sat up, taking quick inventory of herself. She noticed that luckily her black skirt had landed exactly where it should. She had one leg forward, one leg back and knees together. It took about one second to actually fall, but the moment seemed exaggerated in time as she heard the cacophony of gasps, conversations, and even laughter from some teenage boys. But then she heard the one thing she least wanted to hear. Lana.

"That's my baby! Jenny! Jenny! Are you okay!? That's my baby!" Lana screamed as if Jen was bleeding out there on the stage. Her mom sounded so crazy, like out of a mental hospital crazy.

She sat there, dazed, for a half moment, knowing she needed to get up fast. She could hear her mother's voice coming closer and closer. Jen got up as quickly as she could in her skirt and heels and turned and bent down to her mom who was now at the stage.

"Mom! I'm fine. I just fell. I'm okay!" Jen said, trying to keep her voice down yet forceful.

"Jenny! Are you okay? Are you okay??" Lana said, still shouting from the edge of the stage not three feet from Jen onstage.

"Mom! I'm fine. I'm fine. I just fell! Go sit down! I'm fine!"

"Jenny, you're hurt. We have to take you to the doctor," Lana replied, still shouting.

"Mom! I'm fine! Go sit down!" Jen shouted this in an angry tone. She looked up and noticed the entire audience silently staring at them, wide-eyed, many with mouths agape. Jen turned to the audience now: "I'm fine. Thank you. I'm fine. Thanks." Turning to Lana in a restrained voice, she said, "Mom, I'm fine! Go sit down. I'm leaving. I'm fine. I don't need a doctor. I'm leaving!"

At this, Jen turned from the audience and walked toward backstage and the side door that led into the hallway. As she walked away she heard her mom calling, "Jenny," but at least she wasn't yelling anymore. It also sounded like an usher or someone was trying to get her to go sit down, but Jen didn't look back.

There were two stagehands and two actors near the backstage door that led back into the school.. All four were gazing at Jen with interest and one of the actors, with disbelief. Jen looked blankly at them and kept walking. As she turned past the group, she heard one of the boys say in a quiet, high-pitched mocking voice, "That's my baby . . . " followed by a giggle from a girl in the group. Jen slammed the door's metal crash bar and then turned and stared at the boy with anger. The boy froze in a half smile that faded to a straight face.

It wasn't until Jen was striding into the hallway and the door swung shut that she could hear them start laughing again.

The click of her heels down the mint-colored hallway was annoyingly loud. Jen was unsure whether it was the fact she was walking so fast or that she never wore heels that made it so obnoxious. She ducked into a doorway closer to the main hallway when she saw someone coming. It was a middle-aged lady dressed in a striped green shirt and blue floral leggings looking for the restroom. Jen successfully ducked into a doorway and the lady seemed to miss Jen completely. She stood there for a moment and was relieved to hear the next scene beginning from a distance. As she was about to emerge from her doorway, she saw the familiar faces of Morgan, followed by Drake and Zoey exiting the back of the theater. Jen didn't even know they were at the play.

"Oh my gosh that was straight crazy," Zoey said laughing.

"That's my baby! Jenny! That's my baby!" Drake said in a mocking high-pitched tone.

"That was some crazy s——," said Morgan laughing.

"You recorded that right, Morgan?" Zoey asked.

"Yeah that's going to go f—-ing viral," said Drake with a laugh.

"Yeah I got it. I'm posting it now."

"You are literally going to have a thousand hits by tomorrow."

"Play it again."

The three stared at Morgan's phone laughing.

"That's my baby! Jenny, you're hurt we have to take you to the doctor!' "Talk about a total loser moment. Nobody's ever going to talk to her again," Drake said laughing again and again.

"I don't know Drake . . . Morgan here is like best friends with her," Zoey said with eyebrows raised.

"No, I'm not. We're not even friends this year," Morgan said as a matter of fact.

Jen could hear no more. She emerged from the doorway and walked straight past the three who immediately stopped talking. They stood and stared blankly as Jen walked past. Jen only locked eyes with Morgan for a second and said, "I'm glad we're not friends this year Morgan," and walked away.

Morgan said nothing and then as Jen was walking away, "Well, we're not."

Jen kept walking but could hear Drake and Zoey laugh and then Drake say "Jenny, my baby, I think you need to see a doctor." The last thing Jen heard was their laughing before she shoved open the double doors through the next section of the hallway.

Jen felt lightheaded. She felt somehow separate from the person walking down the hallway. Her mind went back to *the moment*. Not the moment on stage in front of everyone but the moment she knew that her life was going to be different than everyone else's.

Chapter 17

She was eleven, eleven and three months to be exact. The age when childhood is in full bloom. When one understands on a juvenile level who they are and what they best appreciate about childhood life. A time when life's carefree indulgences have peaked. Old enough to be able to participate in the pleasures of kid life without the responsibilities of adult life, or the pretensions of adolescence. You were tall enough to ride on roller coasters, not be the smallest kid on the playground and were able to simply enjoy life. Sleepover parties, Lego wars, blanket forts, tea parties, Choose Your Own Adventure books, movies, and video games. It was at this glorious summer of youth that Jen came to a life-altering realization. It was a simple field trip that finally gave it away; the fifth grade end-of-year field trip to Cedar Point amusement park. Jen was so excited to go. It was an overnight trip and each student attending had to pay $105. It was a lot of money for Lana, but luckily, both Jen and Aunt Julie donated some money to go on the trip. Jen had paid the $45 deposit to go on the trip from her own savings. She needed only to bring the remaining $60; the $40 from Aunt Julie and another $20 from Lana. Jen thrice explained this to her mom, but Lana still did not understand how much more she had to give or why. Jen explained again but she still didn't get it. Jen showed her mathematically on paper again and again. Lana still didn't get it. Lana even told Jen she was wrong a couple times. It went on minute after minute of Jen explaining and Lana still not understanding the very basic addition. Jen just stared at Lana in disbelief. Is she kidding? Jen knew she was not.

How was it possible that her mom didn't know this? This was not the only time Jen ever had to correct her mom in basic math. She then thought of every time her mom did something stupid or illogical. Every time she forgot something, every time she messed up a recipe, every time she did something weird or embarrassing, and every time she heard her mom had overdrawn their bank account. Jen sat there in silence. Lana was talking to her but Jen only heard background noise. How had she missed this? Why hadn't she figured this out earlier? It was obvious all along. Jen's thoughts swirled ninety miles an hour in her head:

I am smarter than my mom. I am smarter than my mom! My mom is not as smart as me. For real, I am the one in my house that is the smartest. She is not smart enough to be a mom. I am going to have to make the decisions for our house. My mom is not smart enough. I am smarter than my mom. I probably have been for years. I thought you had to be like in college or something before you're smarter than your parents. I'm eleven. This explains why I argue with her so much. I am smarter. Am I going to be able to make all the decisions for our house? Am I smart enough? What if I'm not smart enough? I have no one to turn to. What if someone tricks me or I mess up? Who will I go to? What will I do if I mess everything up and no one is there to help me? I don't think I'm ready for this. No wonder our family is always poor. We probably lose money because of Mom. I don't think I'm ready. I don't think I'm ready. I'm smarter than my mom. How could I end up with such a dumb parent? Why am I so unlucky? Why me? I am smarter than my mom.

And so her thoughts went. Jen barely slept that night. She thought about all the decisions she might have to make. She thought about how she could have to help her mom be an adult even when she was nowhere near being an adult herself. She thought about how she would have to grow up fast. She thought about how her life would be much different than the life of her friends.

It was so much to bear that Jen's behavior started changing. She began to be defiant to her mom for the first time. She would yell at her mom, and one evening she even called her mom stupid when Lana told Jen she was grounded. To this day, Jen still felt bad about that. For weeks, Jen had problems sleeping. Lana eventually started to notice, but Jen refused to tell her anything. About a month later, Aunt Julie came to visit and took Jen aside to ask what was wrong and that is when Jen broke.

"I'm smarter than my mom! I am, Aunt Julie! There's something wrong with her. I'm not even twelve and I'm smarter than her. I have been for a long time. She doesn't remember things. She doesn't know how to do things. She can't do math. I'm smarter than her."

"Jen, I'm so sorry. I should have told you long ago."

They cried together.

"Aunt Julie, what's wrong with her? Is she like mentally disabled or something?"

"No, your mom was diagnosed with a learning disability. That can mean a lot of things but to your mom it means she has trouble with short term memory, math, and has difficulty interacting with people in social settings. She doesn't understand social cues and tends to speak and act without thinking. Obviously her reading is good which probably kept her from being diagnosed for a long time. When the reading became more difficult and she had to remember more and more information she began to get poor grades. She almost didn't graduate from high school. She never had many friends and never had very good grades. But in high school, both of those things got worse. It wasn't until she was halfway through high school that she got diagnosed for a learning disability. Not that Hemlock Ridge is the worst school system in the world, but your mom sorta fell through the cracks. And it wasn't until a good math teacher suggested that there was a problem and actually went out of her way to get your mom tested, that they did something about it. That at least got your mom through high school."

Jen and Aunt Julie talked for hours as Aunt Julie explained that she didn't want to burden Jen with everything but that she probably should have said something earlier. She also explained that while academically she might be more intelligent than her mom, her mom still deserved respect. Lana had life experience Jen did not have, and she was a good mother despite her shortcomings. Jen admitted that, overall, she was still a good mom.

It was after this that things started to get better. Jen had someone to talk to and Aunt Julie had begun calling Jen from Michigan every two weeks or so ever since just to check up.

But none of that mattered now. Things being slightly better didn't change anything. Jen had been humiliated in front of the whole school, so much so that even her former best friend had to lie to keep from being associated with her. Jen kept walking.

She strode past the "No Entry" sign placed in front of the dark hallway illuminated by only a few exit lights. It looked creepy barely lit. Jen half hoped she would be attacked and put out of her misery. She walked past the last few sets of lockers toward the outer door next to the glass enclosed corner office and exited where there was not a soul in sight.

It had started raining again. The rain was cold, but it didn't matter. Jen was happy for it. Jen wanted to feel the cold, she wanted to feel the pain of cold. She pushed through the rain and stopped at a yellow beech tree past the far corner of auxiliary parking. She leaned up against the tree and screamed, "Why! Why does this all have to happen? Why me?" Jen began crying so hard that she couldn't speak. Add in the shiver from the rain and she had nothing more she could say. Her heels began to sink in the soft ground as she continued leaning against the golden beech tree that was steadily dropping its leaves through the rain. She looked down and for the first time noticed the side of her hand. There was a chunk of skin gone, and blood was dripping as steady as the rain. She must have left a trail all the way down the hallway. She watched it for a minute, and could now feel a throbbing. Rain washed the blood to the ground mixing it into tiny swirling pools on the roots of the tree. She looked up at the orange and yellow leaves floating down through the rain and branches and whispered the word, "Why?" She sat for a moment in absolute silence and blankness.

Then she felt something. She felt the last thing she was expecting. She felt peace. Peace she couldn't explain. Peace that took her into a different moment. It was the same moment but somehow it was now a better moment. Then she felt the Voice. She didn't hear it. It wasn't audible but it was as if someone was speaking from inside her mind. It said: "*I know the plans I have for you. Plans to bless you, Jen, not to hurt you, plans to give you a hope and a future.*" New tears began to fall. Different tears, not of anger, not of pain, but tears of relief. Tears that came from feeling love, love like Jen had never felt before. The feeling was so strong that it somehow felt physical and she even felt it surging through her veins. She didn't know exactly why, but Jen knew that everything was going to be alright. She knew she had heard those words before from Reverend Adam but yet she knew this time they had nothing to do with him. He was the last person on her mind right now. She knew those words were for her. God was speaking to her this time. Jen sat in euphoric peace for a few seconds as her clothes became more and more wet, yet her soul and even her body felt warm and rejuvenated.

The feeling slowly faded until Jen felt nothing but the cold rain. She noticed the last couple dry patches of her clothes absorbing the rain. She looked up at the wet autumn through the red, yellow, and orange trees. It was beautiful but also cold, so cold that Jen got up.

As she rose to her feet, Jen said the most meaningful prayer she had ever said: "Thank You."

Jen started walking back toward the school. She felt nothing, but instead of the empty depressing nothing that was normal to Jen, she felt a calm content nothing. Her hair was now soaked, and the drops seemed to drip straight down the back of her neck causing her to shiver every few steps.

As Jen headed back toward the school, she noticed she was all the way at the edge of what could be considered Hemlock Ridge High School's campus. Jen followed the sidewalk to the main building. As she approached the adjacent faculty parking lot, Jen was happy that the sidewalks were full of puddles but empty of people. She noticed her shoes, which now had only patches of shiny black. The rest of the shoes were now camouflaged with mud, grass, and tiny leaves. *These stupid shoes. What was I thinking?* She shook her head and kept walking.

It occured to Jen that they must have kept going with the show and there would soon be an intermission. Jen wishfully considered that people might forget what happened as the play continued. A young woman was walking ahead. Jen tried not to make eye contact with her, but before she got a chance to turn her head to avoid at her, she heard,

"Jen! Jen, are you okay?"

It was Lindsey Jenkins. Jen looked up and gave a half smile through the soaked hair hanging around her.

"Jen, I'm so so sorry," Lindsey said while wrapping her arms around Jen. Jen was not expecting to be hugged, but it was comforting and much warmer than she had felt a moment ago.

"Are you okay?" Before Jen got a chance to answer, Lindsey began again, "Jen you have to be freezing!" And again before Jen had a chance to respond, she found herself wearing Lindsey Jenkin's very fashionable navy trench style rain jacket. It was warm and had a clean, fresh smelling perfume smell to it. Jen felt a little awkward wearing the jacket but it was so warm that she just went with it.

"Jen, your mom has been looking for you. She's obviously worried. I saw what happened. I'm so sorry, Jen. Are you okay?"

"Yeah, I'm okay I guess." Part of Jen wanted to tell Lindsey about her moment outside, but she didn't know how to tell her so she didn't say anything else.

"So your mom has been a little worked up ever since then. Do you want me to bring her out to you so she's not so worked up in front of anyone else?"

"Yes, thank you," Jen said relieved that Lindsey had thought of that.

Jen stood under the overhang of the nearest entrance to the school. Her soaked hair hung straight down clinging to her ears. Jen saw someone walking through the clear glass enclosure and turned and stepped over to the very edge of the overhang to avoid being seen by anyone walking by. Jen felt like she should be angry, but for some reason she was not. She felt a sort of numb peace. She wasn't sure why, but it was as if her mom, Morgan, and all the embarrassment, self-loathing and anger she had felt didn't matter. Almost like it was a dream but she still wasn't awake yet. She knew her feelings and the sense of peace had something to do with that moment she had with God, but she didn't know what or how. She just calmly stood waiting for Lindsey and her mom to return.

Jen could see her mom coming through the glass enclosure. Lana was walking so fast that she looked as if she was trotting or awkwardly jogging. Although Lindsey was much taller, she looked as if she was straining to keep up with Lana. She burst through the outside door.

"Jenny, Jenny! I thought you were really hurt! Jenny! Don't do that to me! I thought you were really hurt."

Now what Jen wanted to say and actually said ended up being two different things.

She wanted to say something along the lines of what *I* did to *you*? What *I* did to *you*? Are you kidding? You absolutely humiliated me in front of the whole school. People will make fun of me forever because of this. You make my life miserable!

But instead she went easy on her mom. "Mom, I'm fine. You embarrassed me in front of the whole school. I was fine and you yelled across the whole auditorium. I'm not a little baby anymore."

"Jenny I'm sorry. I was worried. I thought you were hurt. I didn't really think about how it could be embarrassing. I was worried you were hurt."

"I was not hurt. It's fine. We have to go. It's almost intermission."

"Don't you have to stay and go back up there?"

"No, I'm done with my lines, and no, I'm not going back out there. Let's go."

Chapter 18

Saturday morning, Jen's eyes fluttered open. Light was pressing through her drawn venetian blinds. Exhausted, Jen did not want to move. She rolled over a little and grabbed her iPod to check the time: 11:33 a.m. *Wow. I really slept in. Lana must be at work.*

She lay in bed for a minute staring blankly up at the ceiling. She felt so out of it, but there was something that she should remember but couldn't. As she lay there half-asleep, she started to realize it wasn't good whatever it was. She started to have a pit in her stomach but her sleepy mind couldn't recall what she was upset about. Her anxiety began to increase. Despite her best efforts to remember, her eyelids started to close again, and she felt herself about to drift off to sleep. Then it flooded back. All at once, she remembered everything: the slip, the fall, Lana screaming, her friends making fun, Morgan telling her they weren't friends, the rain, the moment of peace, everything. Jen's eyes were wide open as she recounted every moment. She wished she could go back to sleep, but her mind was racing, and she was suddenly wide awake.

Jen sat up and pushed back the covers. She looked for her pink flip flops, inserted her toes and noticed her fancy shoes, covered in mud, laying on the floor. She squinted at them in anger, grabbed them, and threw them across the room. *D—— shoes! That's what I get the one time I try to actually look nice.*

As she opened the door to head to the bathroom, whiffs of bacon, syrup, and Lana's buttery, starchy, extra-delicious pancakes hit her nose and initiated hunger that Jen hadn't felt five seconds earlier. Lana often worked Saturday mornings, but obviously wasn't working today. After a quick trip to the bathroom, Jen yawned and walked downstairs. Walking through the living room to the dining room only made the delightful smell increase. There she saw Lana smiling and humming "Moon River."

"Hi Jen!"

"Uh, hi, Mom. You don't have work today?" Jen said, wishing her mom was at work.

"Well, I talked to Amy at work and she was willing to switch with me."

"Okay," Jen said, not wanting to say anything more.

Jen noticed the clock again and figured Lana was trying to make up after everything and let Jen sleep in. Jen wasn't sure if she wanted to be fine with her mom just because she let her sleep in. Just thinking about it still made her feel so out of it, as if her head were in the clouds.

"Well, just eat your breakfast, Honey," Lana said as she handed a plate of delicious buttery pancakes with her famous strawberry maple syrup, whip cream, and a couple of strips of bacon laying parallel on top of the golden brown pancakes.

Jen began to salivate just thinking about the bacon and pancakes. They looked ridiculously delicious. However she wasn't sure if she wanted to eat them; she was still mad about what happened. While Jen was happy to have such a serendipitously tasty breakfast, she didn't want to accept the delicious-looking olive branch when she was still upset. Within moments she gave in.

I can eat pancakes without accepting what my mom did.

Jen's mouth was happy that her brain had arrived at this conclusion. About ten bites into her pancakes, the phone rang.

Lana answered.

"Hello? Oh, hi yes, she is here. Yes. Yes, you may talk to her. She just woke up. She's eating her breakfast. She's eating pancakes and bacon." Jen rolled her eyes. Lana had this habit of giving way too much unnecessary information to people especially while on the phone.

"Jen, it's for you. It's Ms. Collins, *the play director.*" Lana said the last three words in a whisper to give emphasis as if Jen didn't know who she was.

"Okay, mom just hand me the phone. Hello?" Jen answered.

"Hi, Jen, this is Ms. Collins from school."

"Hi, Ms. Collins."

"Hey, I just wanted to say I'm sorry for the other night."

"Yeah, okay, ah well I'm sorry. I'm sorry about what happened," Jen said while getting up from the table in order to distance herself from her mom. Lana started to follow, but then Jen shook her head and put a finger up to motion for her to stay, and Lana did. Jen continued, "Yeah I'm really sorry. My mom, uh, she's hard to explain."

"Jen don't even worry about it. Some of the other students told me about her." Jen rolled her eyes in annoyance. God only knew what the other students had said about her.

"Okay," she responded not knowing what to say next.

"Yeah Jen, I just don't want to stress you or your mom out anymore so I just gave your part to another student for the next two shows. I just wanted to make sure you were okay and I didn't want anything more to upset you or your mom."

"Oh, okay. Thanks," Jen said without enthusiasm.

"You're welcome, Jen! I just want you to be okay."

"Okay, thanks."

"Okay, Jen we'll talk to you again soon, bye."

"Bye."

Almost immediately Lana came from around the corner making it pretty obvious she was eavesdropping. "Jenny, Jenny! What did she want? Is she calling to tell you what a good job you did?"

Jen shook her head.

"No she didn't, Mom. She just told me that I didn't have to come back the next two days. Maybe they think I need rest or something."

"I thought you said you were okay."

"Yeah I am okay, but maybe *they* think I'm not okay."

"Oh, well it's probably best to rest up anyway."

"Yeah, I guess . . ." Jen said with an eyeroll.

"Jenny, I just wanted to say sorry to you for what happened. I wanted to make breakfast for you and spend some time with you."

"Oh, okay well thanks, I guess. I don't know. I don't think you are *able* to understand how embarrassing that was. I just don't understand how you didn't know I was okay. You can't die from slipping and falling! Why did you think I was so hurt? It wasn't a big deal until you started screaming in front of the whole school. I just don't understand you!"

"I don't know Jenny. I . . . I . . . . . . just thought you were hurt. I was worried about you, Jenny! You could have been hurt so bad!"

"No, Mom, I couldn't have. You were the only one in the entire place that thought that."

"Jenny, I think it's going to be okay."

"Will it, Mom?" Will it be okay? Maybe okay for you! Not for me. I'm going to go take a nap. I'm still tired."

"Okay Jenny, I'm sorry. I just want everything to be okay."

"Well, it's not okay," Jen said walked back to her room.

When she got upstairs, she flopped on her bed and put her face into her pillow. She just left her face there for a moment smushed by fluff and pillowcase. She couldn't stop thinking about the call from Ms. Collins. She was so annoyed and offended that she didn't let Jen come back.

Shouldn't that be my decision? Did Ms. Collins think she was fooling me by telling me she was looking out for me and not wanting me to get stressed out, saying I need to rest? I know she just doesn't want me to ruin her precious play again!

The more Jen thought about it, how could she blame Ms. Collins for not wanting *Train Wreck Part 2*?

And how could I recover from that? The next day would be ridiculous. I know I would be so ridiculously nervous. What would I tell Mom? She'd be devastated if I told her she couldn't go, but how could she go? Maybe she deserves to have her feelings hurt. Still, I couldn't imagine what the other cast members would say. Maybe it is a good thing I'm not doing it. Why? Why does my mother have to be like this? She already ruined her own life. Why does she have to ruin mine too?

Almost immediately Jen knew that it was unfair to think her mom had ruined her own life. All in all, Lana's life could be much worse. Jen, however, did not feel bad for thinking that her mom was ruining *her* life, though.

She rolled over, lying there on her back staring up at the ceiling as tears began to roll down the sides of her face. She could feel the pillow on both sides of her face starting to get wet.

The pervasive question in her mind again was *why me?*

But a moment later, that feeling of overwhelming peace came over her again. And into her mind, as if it came from somewhere else:

"*I know the plans I have for you. Plans to bless you, Jen, not to hurt you, plans to give you a hope and a future.*"

Jen felt as if she were hearing anew, not just remembering. She was again overwhelmed by a feeling of love. The only difference was this time the tears stopped when she felt it. She closed her eyes and was asleep moments later.

Jen spent the rest of the day reading, napping, and watching TV until her Aunt Julie called towards dinnertime.

"Jen, your mom told me what happened. How bad was it?"

"Bad."

"Aww, how humiliating! Jen, I'm so sorry!! Jen, I'll come down in a couple weeks and we'll catch up. Hang in there. If we weren't away for the weekend in Traverse City, I would come now!"

"That's okay."

"I'll call you later if I get a minute."

"Okay."

"Okay, Jen I love you. I gotta go."

"I love you too, Aunt Julie."

Jen, Lana, and Ronnie were off to church the next morning. Jen walked into First Congregational Community Church. She looked around for Adam and Lindsey as she did every week. Usually they were the ones that found Jen. Today, Jen looked throughout the service turning her head to the side and even taking glances behind to see if they were somehow sitting in the back, yet Adam and Lindsey were nowhere to be found. Jen had brought the stylish rain jacket Lindsey had lent Jen while she was standing in the rain. Since Lindsey had been at the play, Jen felt Lindsey was one of the few people that understood and might be a good person to talk to. She went back and forth about possibly calling Lindsey to talk but couldn't bring herself to it. She was kind of hoping Lindsey would call her, but it hadn't happened. Although Jen tried to distract herself with homework, books, music, and movies, she still felt like she was on a roller coaster ride, feeling devastated and depressed one moment, oddly numb another, and then almost hopeful toward life in the next.

Chapter 19

Monday was back to school. She had been trying to avoid thinking about school. She had been semi-successful up until last night. She lay awake in bed for hours worrying and then tossed and turned all night until morning. Her first concern was the bus. Luckily, the bus trip ended without anyone saying a word to her.

I wonder if I'm making too big of a deal about it. Maybe in two days time people already forgot. There weren't too many people there. Maybe only a few people know what happened.

As she was entering the building, however, she saw two girls walking about fifteen feet ahead turn and point in her direction. Jen took a quick look behind her. There was a cute boy in a long-sleeved plaid shirt and skinny jeans. Jen tried to convince herself she was overreacting.

You're being paranoid, Jennifer! Jen told herself with fake confidence.

But it wasn't a moment later when two hipster-looking guys entering the school ahead of Jen turned and pointed and said, "My baby," mocking Lana's high-pitched voice, and then busted up laughing and turned in the opposite direction. Jen closed her eyes for a second and slightly shook her head. The embarrassment and pain came flooding back. After the indifferent bus ride, Jen had felt hopeful, but within twenty-five seconds of entering the building, it started. Jen walked towards her locker, following the double row of fluorescent lights that hung from the ceiling. She found it strange that those two guys just happened to be at the play. She remembered looking out and seeing mostly the family of the cast and very few students from her school. And the ones that were there seemed to be mostly girls. As she walked she saw no less than three groups of people pointing at her and laughing while walking in the opposite direction down the hall. Several students looked at their phones and then Jen, back to their phones and then back up at Jen, as if to check if Jen was the same person as on their phones. Then it hit her.

That stupid video! Everyone knows! There could be thousands of people that saw the video! Everyone in the entire school must have seen that video by now.

Jen's heart dropped and her stomach turned to knots. She could almost feel her face flush with color. She knew that part of the reason she had felt detached from what happened is that she didn't have access to social media at her home. Lana was not one of the 99 percent of the world's population who thought of the internet as a necessity. Up until a couple weeks ago, Jen had been using their neighbor's WiFi without a password. Apparently the neighbor got a new internet service and now their internet was password-protected. Jen put her head down and took out her iPod touch and pretended to look through it in order to remain unnoticed. She wished she had her earbuds with her so she could drown out the noise too. She couldn't connect to the school WiFi either because it was only for teachers and school-sanctioned devices. Jen knew she couldn't actually use her iPod to check messages, but she liked that it at least made her appear like she had a phone like everyone else. Jen glanced up every few seconds to make sure she didn't run into the students ahead of her as she walked down the hall, yet she still heard people in high-pitched voices calling, "Jenny, Jenny you need a doctor!" Jen felt sick to her stomach and her head felt spacey.

As Jen stopped at her locker for a minute to grab her stuff, she shook her head and thought: *I wish this locker could absorb me. Or I wish I was small enough that I could step inside and shut myself in. I could hide there and not be seen. Maybe I could just take a nap while standing up. This is where I live now. Okay, maybe not but maybe I can go home sick . . . .*

Her thoughts were interrupted as she saw Mr. Doss coming through the hallway. He was looking at Jen and began walking with pace towards her. It was now clear he was coming to talk to her. Jen pondered the last few days.

I'm not in trouble, am I? Did I do something? Was it because I cussed at those kids? Oh shoot, am I in trouble for real?

Mr. Doss was so large that Jen had to keep tilting her head back and back to look at him when he finally stood before her. Jen was overwhelmed with fear that he was going to yell at her. Mr. Doss was about seven inches taller than the lockers and was about three to four lockers across.

"Ah, Jen, hey I just want to tell you not to listen to those other kids. I saw what happened Friday and I heard them talking already," Mr. Doss spoke with a deep voice that was firm but kind. "Don't let them get to you. Ignore them. These kids walk around here like they're so cool and know everything. They're idiots. They don't know nothing! They ridicule other students because they think that makes them better but it doesn't. High school is short. Before they know it everything is gone and all they did was put others down and they are left with nothing. Don't pay any attention to them. You are a very nice girl and you seem to have a bright future in front of you. Don't let them get you down. And if you ever need anything, don't be afraid to ask me."

Jen stood there for a second. Part of her was annoyed that Mr. Doss already heard students talking about her. However, she was a little encouraged and a lot surprised to hear Mr. Doss speak to her. She hesitated to say something. Mr. Doss looked as if he felt awkward that he had spoken that many sentences to one human at one time. It was by far the most Jen had ever heard him talk.

"Okay. Thank you," Jen said, trying to sound appreciative.

"You're welcome," he said in a very matter-of-fact manner, and with that, Mr. Doss turned and marched off in the opposite direction.

Jen was more than happy when the final bell rang. She rushed out of class and while normally she was annoyed when other students pushed to get out of the doorway, today she was the one bumping into students to get out of the door. Luckily her class had a close exit towards the buses. Jen jogged toward the exit and through the door. She noticed a woman standing near the buses. She realized it was Lindsey Jenkins. Jen remembered the jacket. She definitely didn't have it at school. Lindsey smiled but there was a seriousness in her expression.

"Hey Jen, can we talk for a few minutes?"

"Oh, hey sorry. I don't have the jacket with me."

"Oh, ha yeah not about the jacket. I'm okay. You can keep it for all I care."

"Oh, ok," Jen said not sure if she really meant it but wouldn't be opposed to keeping such a nice jacket.

"Can we go out for some tea this afternoon? I checked with your mom. She said it was fine."

"Oh, okay, yeah. Let me just tell the bus driver to tell Ronnie not to wait for me." Jen yelled up to Betty to tell Ronnie not to wait. She reluctantly agreed but reminded Jen that she wasn't "an answering service."

Turning to Lindsey, she said, "Yeah that's Betty."

"Ha, charming. So Jen I don't really know of any tea places but I heard a local coffee place has good tea. I'm parked over here."

Jen followed Lindsey over to her Honda Civic and hopped in for the short trip to a local coffee spot.

"Wow, it really is called 'The Coffee Coffin.' I thought I misread that when I Googled it," Lindsey said.

"Yeah, apparently it used to be a funeral home and instead of redecorating everything they decided to just go with it and keep all the decor. I've never been there but I hear kids talking about it at school."

"Okay, well I guess we'll see for ourselves."

"Yeah I guess it's like the local hipster hangout or something," Jen said.

"As long as they have good coffee, I could care less."

Sure enough, The Coffee Coffin looked like a funeral home from forty years ago, complete with faded vintage flower wallpaper, but with a coffee bar. The one strange exception was next to the counter and cash register, where one would usually find a table with cream, spoons, lids, sugar, and stirrers, there was a wooden coffin standing upright with shelves inside of it. On the shelves were the usual coffee condiments. It was both funny and creepy; *half and half,* Jen thought. Lindsey ordered a pumpkin spice flat white and Jen ordered the papaya passion fruit tea. After Lindsey ordered and paid, she leaned over to Jen and said,

"Should I be scared to go get a lid?"

"Maybe," Jen said with a giggle.

They sat down at a table with Lindsey facing the door.

"Jen, sorry this is such short notice. There's just something I want to talk to you about. But first, *how are you?*" Lindsey said this last part with seemingly genuine concern. She paused and looked right into Jen's eyes as if she was searching for pain. She continued when Jen hesitated to respond: "Ya know . . . about what happened at the play, I can only imagine how humiliating that would be."

"Yeah." Jen just sat for a moment not sure what to say and not sure how much she wanted to open up about everything she thought. She hadn't really talked to anyone about what had happened. Even though she had wanted to talk to Lindsey, now that she was right there in front of her, she felt stupid talking to her. Lindsey just waited, keeping eye contact. Jen looked down. The silence, while only a few seconds, was starting to get to her.

"I don't know," Jen said with a sigh. "Today was hard. There's a video of it."

"Wait, like someone caught it and put it on YouTube?"

"Yeah, YouTube, Instagram, Tik Tok, Facebook, SnapChat, all of those. I have had lots of people I've never even met before just coming up to me and making fun of me."

"Oh my gosh, Jen, I'm so sorry. I can't even imagine. Wow, that's something I don't envy about growing up now. When I was in high school, the cameras on phones were so bad that the videos recorded either took forever to load or were so blurry that it was almost pointless to try to record video. Now it's crystal clear HD video ready in a half second to record your life's most embarrassing moments. Oh my gosh, Jen I can't even imagine."

"Yeah the worst part about it was that my former best friend recorded it and posted it."

"What? Are you sure?"

"Yeah I overheard her as she was telling the people she was with that we weren't even friends . . . "

"Oh my gosh that's awful!"

"Yeah we've been friends since third grade, but now she has new friends and a new boyfriend or whatever. Yeah, I don't know. I kinda just don't care anymore."

"Jen, I'm so so sorry."

"Yeah, I mean, like it's so annoying. What's wrong with people, ya know? Like, they don't have anything else to do but to make fun of others."

"Yeah, people are like that. They literally will try to find anything they possibly can about you to degrade you in order to feel better about themselves. You're an easy target, so everyone piles on."

"Yeah. Ya know, part of me was scared people would find out about my mom but now everyone knows. I don't have to be scared anymore about that. That was one of my biggest fears coming to high school, but the secret is out. Now it's just dealing with all the annoying students."

"Jen, that's a really mature way to think about it. Not sure I know many ninth graders that think like that, but you're right. It's over. The worst has happened and you're still standing. It's going to get better from here."

"I sure hope so. It doesn't look like that's going to be anytime soon," Jen replied with a sigh.

"You're a special girl, Jen Morris. I think God has big plans for you."

"It's kinda weird to say but I kinda felt like . . . I don't know . . . I guess I felt like God was telling me that or something. Yeah like the day when that happened at the play with my mom, I felt Jesus or God speaking like in my mind."

"Really? Like what do you mean? You felt God speaking to you or something?"

"I don't know I was so angry about everything when it happened. I was just angry-crying in the rain, and all of a sudden, like I had this thought in my mind . . . but it wasn't from me. Somehow I knew it was Jesus and He was going to help me and He had plans for my life."

"Wow. That's incredible Jen. There is nothing like when God fills your heart with His peace," Lindsey paused and looked right at Jen. She looked a little like she was going to cry.

"Yeah, I think I felt that, and still feel it, but not all the time."

"Well, yeah you won't always feel amazing. You'll have some really bad days but we have hope in God, that He will work everything for the good even when we don't feel it."

"Yeah," Jen said thoughtfully. She looked up at Lindsey and she still seemed upset.

"Jen," Lindsey paused and looked down, "Jen there's something I have to tell you. Adam and I are no longer going to be the youth ministers at church."

Jen stared blankly at Lindsey. *Really? I finally have people in my life that I can talk to, and they're gone. Of course.*

"I can't really get into everything that happened and all that, but we're going to be leaving the church. We're going to maybe try to stay in the area or something, but honestly we're not sure what's going to happen."

"Oh," Jen said unsure of what to say.

"Yeah. Jen, I'm so sorry, but don't worry. We'll stay in contact. God has us in each other's lives for a reason. Even if we move away, I'm really good at staying in touch. I even have friends from elementary school still."

"Okay," Jen said, pretending her heart hadn't dropped.

They talked for a few more minutes before Lindsey had to get going. Before she dropped Jen off, she encouraged her to continue praying more since her experience. Jen left Lindsey's car and walked up to her house.

Ok, God, what now? Not sure these good plans for me entail losing people who care about me . . .

Chapter 20

Thursday was better. Jen counted only two people that made fun of her for the infamous video. It had been three weeks since the play. As of last week, the video had over twenty-six thousand views on YouTube alone, which boggled Jen's mind considering there were only about four thousand people who lived in her community. But Thursday, only two people had made fun of her, a new record, breaking Tuesday's record of only three people making fun of her.

Jen picked up the pace as she walked toward the bus. Jen had recently made a habit of getting everything she needed to go home for the day during lunch so she could make a break for it once school was out instead of stopping at her locker to get her things. She didn't want someone ruining her new record with an insult or a joke, but just as she turned the corner to make her way through the last hallway toward the exit she heard a guy's voice yell to her.

"Jen! Hey, Jen!"

Jen almost didn't turn around, but he was actually calling her by name, and not "My Baby" or "girl with the mental mom" or any number of the degrading adaptations that other students called her in the lunchroom or hallways away from any teachers that might stick up for her. She turned and saw one of the guys that went to youth group. Dylan and his friend Francisco were a couple of the guys Reverend Adam met at the park. They had begun coming to youth group every week. As Jen turned and Dylan walked up to her, she caught a whiff of smoke or some kind of incense. It wasn't fresh but smelled as if he had washed his clothes in burnt leaves the day before.

"Jen! Hey did you hear about that D-bag reverend dude at the church? He like fired Adam and Lindsey!"

"No, really? Lindsey told me they were leaving the church, but she never told me why."

"Yeah one night I overheard the reverend all yelling at Adam cause he showed us his shoulder tattoo and he started saying that all the kids like us that started coming were bad influences on the church and how we cuss and stuff and we were going to lead the people of the church astray and all this bull s—-."

"Really?"

"Yeah and then like two weeks after that Adam is like fired. It makes me mad! Adam and Lindsey were chill AF."

"Yeah that's stupid. I had no idea."

"Yeah bro I'm pissed!"

Jen paused for a moment. *Really? "Bro?" Well, I guess it's better than a lot of the names I've been called the last few weeks.*

"Yeah that sucks. Hey, I gotta grab my bus. I'll talk to you later Dylan."

"K. Deuces."

As she walked to the bus, all she could do was think about how Reverend Shepherd fired Adam and Lindsey.

Typical, the only people that ever attended church that were actually cool got fired. It makes me not want to go to church ever again.

Jen walked back to her seat and sank down, burying her face in the green vinyl. Jen was ready for the day to be over and to go take a nap before Lana got home. She turned slightly towards the window as not to look at any other students that came on the bus. In a perfect world, she would have sat in the front as she was one of the first stops but she knew that the annoying students from the intermediate school including her brother Ronnie were going to be entering and sitting towards the front, so the middle would have to suffice. Jen was trying not to pay attention to the guys coming onto the bus. Part of her was hoping that none of them would remember to make fun of her and as they had done many times the last couple weeks. She sat slumped down, turned toward the window and pulled her hood up. Her backpack was propped up on her right shoulder making a mini-wall, as she stared left out the window pretending not to pay attention, even though she was listening to every word, hoping that if the bus riders didn't notice Jen, the taunting wouldn't occur. As much as Jen was beginning to grow immune to it, she looked forward to the day when the teasing would cease altogether and become yesterday's news.

She heard the steps first. They were more like stomps than steps.

"Whatever, shut up!" said an adolescent male voice.

"I will not. It's not my fault you can't get a date," added another sassy female. "I really can't blame her, though. You are annoying AF."

"Yeah he is!" called another male voice.

"Guys shut the hell up, will ya?" said the first voice in frustration.

"Hey! What I tell yinz about language on my bus?" Everyone froze in shock from Betty's sudden interjection.

"Sorry."

"Sorry, Ma'am."

"Sorry, Betty."

"Sit down!"

As the students turned to sit down, the girl saw Jen and hesitated for a moment. She stood at her seat staring at Jen as if she was trying to figure her out. Jen caught a glimpse of her out of the corner of her eye but couldn't really make out who it was.

"Hey, I'm Sophia," she finally said.

Jen turned and realized that it was the girl she'd met in the bathroom after that rough day of play practice.

"Oh, hey, I'm Jen."

"Yeah, I remember you. From the bathroom, right?"

"Yeah. Maybe not my best moment, but yeah."

"Nah, I thought you were cool."

"Ha, yeah I guess . . . "

"Hey is anyone sitting here?"

"Um. No," Jen said, suddenly surprised that someone had asked to sit with her.

"Okay, cool thanks. I'll sit here then. I didn't know that you rode the bus with my loser cousin."

"Oh yeah," Jen said, trying to sound unbothered by the intrusion of her seat.

Sophia plopped down on the seat next to Jen with an army green backpack that had patches on it. One said "Crazed and Confused." A whiff of Sophia's perfume, which smelled like an oddly pleasant mixture of soap, flowers, and bug spray, filled the seat.

"How's it going?" Sophia said, adjusting her backpack on her lap and leaning back.

"Fine," Jen said, nodding her head unsure of what to say to the girl she really didn't know.

"Hey, I wanted to ask you something. So, are you the girl in that video with the mom that yells out at the play or whatever?"

"Yeah," Jen said with a sigh.

"Oh, okay. Yeah, I was just curious. I thought it was you."

"Yeah, it is me. It's super embarrassing, and I wish people would find something to do other than watch videos of my crazy mom."

"Yeah, I saw it. I don't get the big deal. So what? Your mom yells a little crazy-like in front of people? Big deal."

"Yeah, I know, but you don't know what it's like all the time. It's not just that. It makes me think of all the other stuff with my mom," Jen said with an eye roll.

Obviously she has no clue what it's like.

"Yeah, but at least your mom cares about you! I would take that over my stupid junkie mom! She loves me and my brother almost as much as she loves drugs."

Jen was taken aback, unsure whether Sophia was telling some sort of weird joke or just being very honest to someone she really didn't know. An awkward "Oh." was the only thing that she thought to say in reply.

"Sorry, I guess that's weird that I just said that. But it's the truth. And the truth sucks. That's what I'm saying about your mom. I mean, maybe she's a little strange but at least she cares about you."

"You don't think your mom cares about you?"

"She says she does, but then she goes and wrecks our family in order to do more drugs."

"Yeah, but I heard that it's like a sickness like anything else. Addiction. Ya know like you have to go to rehab and see a doctor."

"Well, let's just say that it's a good thing I'm better at school than my mom is about rehab."

"That sucks."

"My mom once showed up to a parent teacher conference completely high as f—-! I had to tell my teacher that my mom had been in the hospital and that she was on medication. Truth is my mom had been gone for two days, and I had no idea where she had been."

"Wow, crazy."

"So be thankful for your mom even if she acts a little crazy now and then."

"Yeah."

"It's crazy. In my house I literally have to be like the grown-up. I have to pay bills and everything. It's nuts."

"Really? Yeah, I do that in my house too."

"Really?"

"Yeah."

"Wow, I thought I was the only one. Huh."

"Yeah, it sucks having to be the grown up and everything in your house."

"Yeah, like I have to always fight with my mom to let me do the bills so they get done right," Sophia said shaking her head in annoyance.

"Crazy. Yeah, for me, at this point, my mom knows that I can do them better than her so she doesn't even fight me about it anymore."

"That's good. I wish my mom would do that with me. Instead I have to fight with her about it and she like yells at me like she knows what she's doing but she doesn't. She yells at me if I do one thing wrong when she does it wrong every time. My brother and I are at my weirdo cousin's house the next couple days while my mom tries rehab for the fourth time." At this, Sophia looked

Jen right in the eyes almost as if to find an answer to a question she didn't ask.

Jen returned her glance. "I'm so sorry, Sophia."

A pair of tears trickled down Sophia's face. Although Jen still didn't really know Sophia, she felt like she needed to encourage her. She suddenly felt empowered to tell her all the things she wished she could tell herself. She felt warm and had goosebumps as she began to speak.

"Ya know what, Sophia? She's lucky to have you as a daughter, because you actually care. You are strong enough to handle this whether you feel like it or not. You can do this! There are so many kids who don't care about anything, but you care enough to support your whole family. You have a heart strong enough to do this. It will get better. Your mom is going to get better, I don't know why I believe this, but I do. One day she will thank you for how you held everything together and for still caring about her. God sees everything you do . . . and . . . and He has plans for your life too! And you can do it . . . and . . . and.." at this Jen had to stop and catch her breath because there were so many words that came out at one time. That was the most she'd spoken to another human person for weeks. She could see the pair of tears had turned into dozens on Sophia's face.

In her best voice through tears, Sophia said, "That . . . was . . . " she paused to cough. " . . . exactly what . . . I needed to hear."

Jen paused and then whispered, "Me too, I think."

Sophia grabbed Jen and did her best to hug her sitting beside her between backpacks and green vinyl seats. Sophia's wet cheek pressed against Jen's and her soft pink and purple hair tickled Jen's nose and made her giggle. As they embraced they were swayed forward as the bus came to a halt, and they let go.

"Well, I gotta go, this is my stop."

"Bye. And Jen . . . " Sophia looked right into Jen's eyes as she and Jen stood pausing to say goodbye, "Thanks." Something about the way Sophia said it made the word seem to have more meaning than it typically has.

Jen smiled and walked down the rubber grooved center aisle. She caught herself in the mirror wearing a big smile. She attempted for a moment to push the smile away but found herself again smiling a moment later. Ronnie even noticed.

"Jen, what are you so happy about?" he asked in a legitimately curious tone.

"Ah, I . . . I . . . don't know. I think I just helped that girl," Jen said, ending her sentence in another smile.

"That's good, Jen. It feels good to help people," Ronnie said with an intonation that was more asking than telling.

"Yeah it does," Jen said, continuing her smile. Jen walked up the drive past rose bushes and broken cement. She felt a little exhausted like she'd given a tiny bit of her soul away, yet rejuvenated. She recalled how her body felt after a good workout, tired yet filled with accomplishment. Jen glanced up at the sun and clouds and felt that the world was a slightly better place.

Epilogue

The following weeks began to go a little better still. Jen's infamous video got more and more views, but the week before Christmas break, the video hit the 35,000 mark. Some of Jen's teachers finally became aware of the video and considered it bullying when other students made fun of Jen in class. While she knew it was her fault she was too embarrassed to say anything to the teachers earlier, she still found it ridiculous that it took teachers that long to finally see and do something about the video, especially since many times students watched it at the end of class. Once she saw students share the video with a teacher who gave a quick laugh and then said nothing more. So while there wasn't a day that went by that Jen wasn't made fun of at least once or twice, it was still an improvement on the half dozen or more times which was frequent before this, and it gave her a hope that after Christmas break it would be better still.

Adam and Lindsey ended up moving to another local area church. At first, Lana was hesitant about letting Jen go to a different church for youth group, but Lana's love of Adam and Lindsey eventually persuaded her. Jen felt so strange trying to convince her mom to let her go to church. The church was a little newer and livelier than her mom's church, even though it was still a church. Jen still met a few annoying, judgemental adults and even some other high schoolers too, but it was overall a very enjoyable experience. She actually looked forward to going every week, especially with Sophia.

Jen and Sophia grew closer in the weeks after they first sat together on the bus. They had a lot in common, and they grew even closer when Sophia and her mom moved in with their cousin on Jen's bus route. While Sophia may have been a little less cool and a little more crazy than Morgan, she was seemingly more loyal. Sophia didn't care who the person was. If she heard anyone making any comments toward Jen, she stood up for her. Morgan tended to only do that if it was obvious that she was more popular than the person making fun of Jen. Jen didn't even really invite Sophia to youth group. Sophia asked Jen what she was doing one day and when Jen told her she was going to a church group. Sophia told her that she was coming too. And she came. Sophia loved youth group and Adam and Lindsey. She told them that they were her new aunt and uncle and she even began calling them Uncle Adam and Aunt Lindsey.

For weeks, Jen hadn't seen Morgan. The opening night of the play had been the last time. Then one Thursday in January, Morgan walked into her lunch period to talk to a couple of her friends. Jen saw her right away, sitting three tables over. She sat and watched wondering how she was and if she was enjoying her life without her. A moment later Morgan noticed Jen looking at her. Surprised that Morgan noticed her, she looked away for a moment only to glance back a second later. Morgan was looking back but instead of the dirty look she was expecting, Jen saw a sort of a blank, contemplative look. Jen stared back inquisitively, nervously wondering if Morgan was going to come over and talk to her. Two seconds later, a friend came over and Morgan got up and left without another glance. The moment left Jen wondering if there was a part of Morgan that wished they were still friends.

With Lana, Jen began to make an attempt to be more kind and understanding. She knew that she wasn't horrible to her mother but she also knew that she could do better. She knew she needed to try a little harder. At Lindsey's suggestion she even prayed that God would help her to think a little more about what her mom was thinking even if it was often hard to decipher.

One cold evening in February, Lana spoke to Jen about what she had been seeing in her.

"Jenny, I don't know what it is but I think you're happier than you have been in a long time."

"Yeah, you think so?"

"Yeah I do."

"It's like you're not trying so hard anymore. Like you're less worried about everything being so perfect."

"Yeah, I guess," Jen said, a little taken aback by her mom's sudden deep insights.

"It's like you now know everything's going to be okay."

"Yeah, I didn't really think about it, but yeah I think you're right."

"I know I'm right. I'm your mother."

"Ha, okay mom," Jen said, laughing affectionately at her mom's confidence.

Maybe, I am the right person for my life afterall.

THE END